BLACKFOOT AMBUSH

"There!" Pike said, and started running for cover. The Indians hadn't spotted them, and wouldn't if they could make it to the thicket.

But Big John Ledger was slow of foot and clumsy. Pike had made it to the thicket with time to spare, but Ledger had either stepped into a hole or stumbled over his own feet, because now he had fallen into the water, losing his rifle. Ledger was about to get to his feet and head for the thicket when Pike heard the Blackfoot call out and he knew they had spotted the large white man.

There were easily a dozen Indians, but it still took them fifteen minutes to overcome Ledger. Finally they rendered the big man unconscious.

"Kill him," Pike prayed softly.

It was a silent plea for the Indians to kill Ledger quickly, but Pike knew that would not happen.

Even now they were dragging Ledger onto dry ground and building a large fire.

EDGE by George G. Gilman

#5 BLOOD ON SILVER (17-225, $3.50)
The Comstock Lode was one of the richest silver strikes the world had ever seen. So Edge was there. So was the Tabor gang—sadistic killers led by a renegade Quaker. The voluptuous Adele Firman, a band of brutal Shoshone Indians, and an African giant were there, too. Too bad. They learned that gold may be warm but silver is death. They didn't live to forget Edge.

#6 RED RIVER (17-226, $3.50)
In jail for a killing he didn't commit, Edge is puzzled by the prisoner in the next cell. Where had they met before? Was it at Shiloh, or in the horror of Andersonville?

This is the sequel to KILLER'S BREED, an earlier volume in this series. We revisit the bloody days of the Civil War and incredible scenes of cruelty and violence as our young nation splits wide open, blue armies versus gray armies, tainting the land with a river of blood. And Edge was there.

Available wherever paperbacks are sold, or order direct from the Publisher. Send cover price plus 50¢ per copy for mailing and handling to Pinnacle Books, Dept.17-341, 475 Park Avenue South, New York, N.Y. 10016. Residents of New York, New Jersey and Pennsylvania must include sales tax. DO NOT SEND CASH.

MOUNTAIN JACK PIKE

#5 GREEN RIVER HUNT

JOSEPH MEEK

PINNACLE BOOKS
WINDSOR PUBLISHING CORP.

PINNACLE BOOKS

are published by

Windsor Publishing Corp.
475 Park Avenue South
New York, NY 10016

First printing: April, 1990

Printed in the United States of America

For Jory Sherman,
thanks for the friendship,
and the encouragement.

Prologue

When they saw the Indians they knew they were in trouble.

"Blackfeet?" Big John Ledger asked.

"Looks like," Jack Pike said. "Better find cover."

They had been trapping the area for weeks, along the Salmon River, Godin's River, Henry's Fork of the Snake River, Pierre's Fork, Lewis' Fork, and the Muddy. They had set this particular batch of traps on a little creek running out of the pass which leads to Pierre's Hold. They were checking them for the first time, and running into a bunch of Blackfoot Indians was something less than a pleasure.

Looking for cover, they spotted a thicket on the other side of the creek.

"There!" Pike said, and started running for it. The Indians hadn't yet spotted them, and if they could make it to the thicket they wouldn't.

Pike could hear Big John Ledger splashing behind him. He was much larger than even Pike's six-four, outweighing Pike by a good fifty pounds, and he was slow of foot and clumsy. Pike made it to the thicket with time to spare, but Ledger had run into trouble. He had either stepped into a hole or stumbled over his own big feet, but Ledger went sprawling into the water, losing his rifle. He groped about for the gun, found it and got to his feet. He was about to head for

7

the thicket again when both he and Pike heard the Blackfeet call out, having spotted him.

"Come on," Pike said softly, urging Ledger to run, but he knew the big man would not. To run for the thicket now would give it away as a hiding place, and since Pike was already there out of sight, Ledger would not want to expose him.

Instead, the big man turned and faced the oncoming Blackfeet. Pike watched as Ledger raised his rifle and pulled the trigger, but the water had wet the powder. Ledger reversed the rifle to use as a club and waded into the charging Indians.

There were easily a dozen Indians and it still took them a good fifteen minutes to overcome Ledger. A couple of them wouldn't live to tell the tale, and several others had taken damaging blows from Ledger's rifle, but finally they had him down on the ground and started doing some damage with their own rifle butts, finally rendering the big white man unconscious.

"Kill him," Pike said softly. It was a silent plea for the Indians to kill Ledger quickly, but Pike knew that would not happen. Even now they were dragging Ledger onto dry ground and building a fire.

They would torture him until he could take no more, and Pike knew that would take a good long while with a man like Ledger.

And he was going to have to lie there and listen to it.

While the Indians were readying Ledger for torture, Pike hurriedly dug himself a foxhole, then settled himself into it. He didn't want to take a chance on watching them, as they might spot him in the thicket. Besides that, he did not want to watch Ledger die. It was bad enough, he knew, that he was going to have to listen to it.

Of course, he could have stood up and tried to help Ledger, but he would only succeed in getting *himself* tortured and killed. Ledger had given himself up to help Pike remain hidden. For Pike to get himself killed would mean that Ledger died for nothing.

At the sound of the first scream, a chill ran down Pike's back.

It was early morning when the Blackfeet took Ledger, and for the remainder of the day Pike tried to drown out the screams of his friend, but it just wasn't possible.

Lying in the damp foxhole all day, Pike soon contracted a steady chill, and slowly a fever built inside of him. By dawn the fever was raging, and he no longer knew if he was actually hearing Ledger scream, or just hearing screams.

Soon, he didn't hear anything at all, real or imagined.

When Pike woke he lay still, trying to remember where he was. Slowly, he staggered to his feet before he remembered that he was hiding from the Blackfeet. Luckily, the Blackfeet had left the night before, leaving behind a lifeless hunk of meat that had once been Big John Ledger.

Pike picked up his rifle and walked across the creek to see his friend. They had taken Ledger's fingers, his eyes and ears, his nose — Christ, his *lips* — they had even cut off his penis. How he could have lasted through all of that, Pike didn't know. He wasn't even sure he was seeing something that was real. He could feel the fever burning behind his eyes, and his flesh was alternately hot and cold.

"I'm sorry, John," he said to the thing at his feet. He knew that he didn't even have the strength to try and bury his friend. To even attempt it would use up what little strength he had and there was always his

9

own survival to look after.

He turned away and walked down the creek, away from the body which had already attracted flies. He knelt at the water's edge and bathed his face and neck with its icy coldness. He was trying to bring his fever down, at least to the point where he could think straight. Finally, he removed his shirt and bathed his upper body. He felt chilled to the bone but found that he was able to focus his thoughts.

The first thing he had to do was look around and see if the Indians had taken their mules and horses. If they had, then he was on foot and would have to make the best of it.

It didn't take him long to discover that he was, indeed, afoot, and now he tried to think of the closest place he could go for help.

Vaguely, he recalled that he was supposed to meet his friend, Skins McConnell, somewhere. Thinking very hard he finally dredged up the name of Bonneville's Fort on the Green River. On a horse he'd be able to make it in three days, easily.

He didn't know how long it would take him to walk, but he knew he'd better get started. He knew the fever would come back, and if he didn't keep moving it would overcome him.

With a last look at Big John Ledger, he started in what he figured was the direction of Bonneville's Fort.

Skins McConnell was worried.

Pike was not only late meeting him, he was *ten days* late, and that was not like him.

He was saddling his horse, readying himself to go out looking for his friend.

"You sure you don't want some help?" "Whiskey" Sam Benedict asked him.

"We ain't got nothing better to do," Rocky Victor

added.

Benedict and Victor were true old timers. They were each in their sixties, and with gray hair and beards. They also had dark, leathery skin from years of exposure. They both wore old skins, and it was usually a toss-up as to which had bathed last.

"No," McConnell said, "I'll go alone. If he ran into Blackfoot trouble three of us will bring them down on us. I can travel better and faster alone."

Both Benedict and Victor understood that this was not a reference to their advanced ages.

"If he ran into Blackfeet," Whiskey Sam said, "it's them that's got the trouble."

"Right," Victor said. "Pike's a hellion, we all know that."

McConnell knew better than anyone what a hellion Pike was. Pike had once ridden into a Crow camp, taking on five Crow alone because they had raped a woman friend of his. He had also been known to tackle a bear on his own. He was a man who was not afraid to bite off more than his share, and one of these days he was going to get himself killed.

McConnell hoped that that day had not come and gone.

He was about to mount up when he heard a shout from outside the fort.

"Man approaching on foot!"

He exchanged a glance with both Benedict and Victor, and then the three of them were running for the gate.

"Wait—" someone said as McConnell started to open it, but they didn't listen and swung the gate wide, running outside.

McConnell saw him, stumbling, trying to keep his balance, falling and getting up and falling again. He reached Pike just as the man had gotten to his feet again, and caught him as he fell.

11

Benedict and Victor came up behind him as he cradled his friend in his arms.

"How is he?" Whiskey Sam asked.

"Wrung out," McConnell said, "and feverish."

"Well," Victor said, "at least he's alive."

"Help me get him inside," McConnell said, "and we can try and keep him that way!"

Part One

Trouble At The Fort

Chapter One

When Pike woke he sat up quickly and looked around him. Before his head started to spin he saw that he was in a room somewhere, lying in a real bed, and then he had to lie back down or pass out.

"You're awake," a woman's voice said.

He turned his head and tried to focus on her. He could smell her before he could see her, and he liked the smell, fresh and sweet at the same time.

She came close to the bed, into focus — more or less. Things were still a little fuzzy around the edges, but he had no problem seeing that she was blonde, the hair long and cascading over one shoulder as she leaned over him. Her skin was clear and unlined, her eyes blue, a startling blue that he had never seen before. She appeared to be in her late twenties.

"How do you feel?"

"Like I died and went to heaven," he said. "Are you an angel?"

"I am if you want me to be," she said, smiling. Her mouth was wide, her lips full and her teeth very white.

She put her hand on his forehead and it felt cool and firm to him.

"Your fever is down," she said. "You don't know how lucky you are."

"Yes," he said, "I do."

He stared at her and was surprised to see her blush

and look away for a moment. He decided to take her off the hook.

"Where am I?"

She looked at him again and said, "Bonneville's Fort—where were you trying to be?"

"Here," he said, "but if I had known you were here I would have tried harder."

She blushed again but didn't turn away.

"You appear to be much better," she said. "Your friend would like to see you."

"Who?"

"Mr. McConnell."

"Skins," he said, "send him in, will you?"

"Surely."

"And see if he can't bring a drink in with him, will you?"

"We'll see," she said, noncommittally. He watched her as she walked to the door, opened it and disappeared.

He was afraid that if he closed his eyes he'd find out when he opened them again that this was a dream, or a hallucination. Maybe he was still back there in that foxhole, and maybe Big John Ledger was still screaming like a banshee as the Indians cut off his—

"Pike!"

He turned his head and saw Skins McConnell approaching the bed. The woman was not with him.

"How do you feel?" McConnell asked.

"Weak," Pike said, "and thirsty."

"There's water here," McConnell said, reaching for it. "I can bring you something stronger later."

"Water will do fine for now."

McConnell poured water into a cup from a pitcher and helped his friend drink it.

"Thanks."

"What happened, Pike?" McConnell asked. "Can you tell me? Can you remember?"

"I wish I didn't remember," Pike said, and told his

16

friend what had happened.

"I should have done something to help him," he finished.

"And you would have gotten yourself killed," McConnell said. "That would have put you *and* Big John in the hereafter, and if he saw you there he would have kicked your butt."

"And he could do it, too," Pike said.

McConnell doubted that, but said nothing.

"How did I get here?" Pike asked.

"You don't remember?"

"No."

"You walked," McConnell said. "Must have taken you close to two weeks. It's a miracle you made it, holding a fever for that long."

"When did I get here?"

"Two days ago. You been in and out since then. In fact, we talked once before, but not this long."

Pike frowned and said, "I don't remember. Who is the girl who was in here?"

"Her name's Sandy," McConnell said, "and she's the closest thing to a doctor here at the fort."

"Did I see her before?"

"Yep."

"And I don't remember her?"

"That must have been some fever you had, huh, for you not to remember a gal like that?"

"Tell me about it," Pike said. He threw off the sheet that was covering him just as the door opened and Sandy entered the room.

"What are you doing?" she asked.

"I'm getting up," he said. "Any objections?"

She crossed her arms in front of her and said, "No, go ahead."

As she watched he got his feet to the floor and stood up — and suddenly he couldn't feel the floor anymore. It was as if it had fallen away from him, and then he started to fall . . . and McConnell caught him and low-

17

ered him onto the bed again.

Sandy came forward and said, "Now that you've gotten that out of your system, would you please lie down again?"

"Yes, Ma'am," Pike said. He laid back and she covered him with the sheet again.

She looked at McConnell then and said, "I think that will be all for now, Mr. McConnell."

"Yes, Ma'am," McConnell said. "I'll see you later, Pike."

"Don't forget to bring me something to drink other than water."

McConnell threw Sandy a wary glance and said, "I'll try."

"Out, please," Sandy said.

McConnell made for the door and escaped.

Pike looked at Sandy again, this time without the fuzzy borders. Everything looked the same as before, but much better.

"Am I going to live?" he asked.

"It would seem so," she said, touching his forehead once again.

"I want to thank you for saving my life, then," he said to her.

"It wasn't me," she said.

"Who was it, then?"

"You."

"Me?"

She put her hand on his chest and said, "This wonderful constitution of yours," and then removed her hand hurriedly, as if his flesh had burned her. She was blushing again. "I mean, you're in such marvelous shape—"

She rose and moved away from the bed, looking away from him.

"Well, I'll thank you for caring for me, anyway," he said, "if you don't mind."

"No," she said, "of course I don't mind . . . and

18

you're welcome." She turned and looked at him again, "You'd better get some sleep. You're not out of the woods by any means."

"All right," he said, "I'll sleep, but only if you promise to be here when I wake up."

She smiled at him and said, "I'm not going anywhere, Mr. Pike."

She started for the door and he said, "By the way . . ."

"Yes?"

"I know your first name," he said, "but what's your last name?"

"Jacoby," she said, "Sandra Jacoby, but you can just call me Sandy."

"And you can call me—"

"Pike," she said, finishing for him. "I've heard that everyone just calls you Pike."

"That's right."

"You'd better go to sleep, Pike," she said. "You'll feel a lot better if you do."

As she left, Pike figured he felt pretty good right then. He didn't know how he had made it to Bonneville's Fort alive and in one piece—unless it was what Sandy Jacoby said about his wonderful constitution.

As he drifted off he thought he could still feel her hand on his chest.

The next time Pike woke he found himself looking at the faces of Whiskey Sam and Rocky Victor. Behind them was Skins McConnell. Sandy Jacoby was nowhere to be seen at the moment.

"She lied to me," he croaked.

"What?"

Pike pointed to the water on the table next to him. McConnell poured him a glass and handed it to him. After a few swallows Pike tried again.

"I said she lied to me."

19

"Who?" Whiskey Sam asked.

"Sandy."

Sam turned to Victor and said, "Who's Sandy?"

"His nurse," Rocky Victor said.

"Oh, the blonde one?" Whiskey Sam said, and Victor nodded.

"How did she lie?" McConnell asked.

"She said that if I went to sleep I'd feel better."

"And?"

"If you woke up to these three faces," Pike asked, "would *you* feel better?"

Whiskey Sam smiled, which was no great pleasure to see, either.

"You would," he said, "if one of these faces had a bottle of whiskey?"

"And do you?" Pike demanded.

Still smiling Whiskey Sam brought up his right hand. In it he held a bottle of whiskey. The bottle had no label, and was probably some homemade brew, but Pike wasn't in any position to complain.

"Gimme," he said, holding out his empty water glass.

Whiskey Sam poured him two fingers and, since there were no other glasses in the room, took a swig and then passed the bottle around.

Pike took a drink and close his eyes as the rotgut burned its way down.

"How long before you're on your feet?" Skins McConnell asked.

"By my reckoning, or Sandy's?"

"Oh, it's Sandy, is it?" Whiskey Sam said knowingly.

"You know Pike's always had a way with the ladies," Rocky Victor said.

"I haven't had my way with anyone," Pike said, scolding the two of them. He looked at McConnell and said, "If I have my way I'll be up and out of here by tomorrow."

"And her way?"

Pike scowled and said, "She'd like to keep me in this bed a few more days."

"She'd like to keep you in bed, eh?" Whiskey Sam said grinning.

"Sam, do me a favor, don't grin like that?"

"Why not?"

"It's scary."

The others laughed. Sam frowned, reclaimed the bottle, took another drink and then cradled the bottle in his arms as if to say he wasn't going to share it any more.

Pike finished off his two fingers and decided that was plenty for him. As far as he was concerned, Whiskey Sam could have the rest. What he really wanted now was a cold beer.

"You fellows will have to leave now," a woman's voice said.

McConnell, Whiskey Sam and Rocky Victor all turned and looked behind them in surprise. None of the three of them had heard Sandy Jacoby enter the room.

She moved closer to them and said to McConnell, "It looks like I'm making a habit out of kicking you out of here."

"Yes, Ma'am," McConnell said, "we was just leaving. Pike, we'll see you tomorrow."

"Right," Pike said.

Whiskey Sam and Rocky Victor waved and followed McConnell out. Sam was still cradling his bottle.

Sandy approached the bed, took the glass from Pike's hand and sniffed it. Her eyes widened and she pulled the glass away.

"That's vile," she said.

Pike smiled, the whiskey still burning his gut and said, "Imagine how I must feel—I drank it."

Chapter Two

Derek Simpson nursed his beer with a scowl on his face. The three men sitting with him — Phil Brick, Al Nudger, and Ed Graves — were not concerned with the scowl. They had known Derek Simpson anywhere from six months to seven years, and as long as they had known him he had worn that scowl. It meant he wasn't satisfied with the way his life was going.

Derek Simpson was *never* satisfied with the way his life was going.

He was forty-two, tall and rangy, balding, with the beginnings of a paunch at his waist. As usual, he was down to his last dollar, as were the others. It never occurred to them that as long as they had ridden with Simpson they always seemed to be down to their last dollar. The two things just never connected up for them. If they *had* thought about it, they might have decided to go their own ways.

On the other hand, Derek Simpson knew that as long as they had been riding together he seemed to be down to his last dollar, but he also knew that it was his doing, not theirs. Splitting from them would not change that fact for him, although it might have changed it for them. He always knew that when *he* was down to *his* last dollar, he could always con them out of *their* last dollar.

So, in reality, while each of them was down to their

last dollar, Derek Simpson was down to his last *four* dollars.

Whatever the case, Simpson was scowling into his beer, but that didn't worry Brick, Nudger and Graves. They knew that Simpson would come up with some kind of plan to make some money for them.

He always did.

They also knew that his ideas were almost always illegal, but that didn't bother any of them. If his plan was legal, it probably wouldn't pay as well.

"I'm going for a walk," Simpson said, pushing his half finished beer away. The others grabbed for it, but Graves was the fastest.

They watched as Simpson left the saloon. They knew that when he decided to go for a walk it was to work out the last details of whatever his plan was. When he came back, he'd tell them what the plan was, and then they could start figuring out how they were going to spend the money they were going to make.

Derek Simpson wasn't just going for a walk, he was going for a walk over to Lottie McCullers's. Lottie ran four whores at the fort, all four of whom Derek Simpson had used at one time or another. Right now he felt like having that little dark-haired squaw girl, the Nez Perce girl that Lottie had found, raised and turned into a mighty fine little whore.

Simpson's reasons for wanting the Indian girl were not totally sexual. His plan for making money had a lot to do with the Nez Perce Indians, and he wanted to find out as much about them as he could.

Who better to ask than a Nez Perce squaw?

He did have one problem, though. He didn't have the price of a whore. Luckily, Lottie collected *after* the fact, and not before, so Simpson decided to worry about paying after the deed was done.

23

Worrying about it before took a lot of the enjoyment out of it.

"Whataya think he's got in mind this time?" Graves asked. He was nursing the remainder of Simpson's beer while the other two looked on thirstily.

"Who knows?" Phil Brick asked. "You never know what Simpson's gonna come up with."

Al Nudger, who had known Simpson the longest, said, "Don't worry about it. Whatever it is, there'll be some money in it."

"Some" money, to Graves, Brick and Nudger, was relative. Since they rarely had more than a dollar or two on them, if Simpson told them they were going to come out with twenty dollars each, that would seem like a lot of money to them. Simpson knew this, and never missed a chance to cheat the three men. Of the three, Nudger was the only one who knew for sure he was being cheated, but he also knew that without Simpson he wouldn't have *any* money to be cheated out of. He was better off with what Simpson let him have than what he could get alone.

Phil Brick had known Simpson—and the others—only six months. He was the youngest of the pack, in his early twenties, and he thought Simpson was the smartest, slickest man he'd ever met.

Ed Graves had known Simpson for three years, and Nudger the same length of time. Simpson and Nudger had been riding together when he met them. Graves was thirty-five, but he looked like the oldest of the bunch because he was so thin and had lost his hair a long time ago. He was also the shortest of the four, the only one who didn't top six feet.

The thirty-seven year old Nudger—at six-foot six—was the tallest and most powerful of the group. He usually weighed about three hundred and ten or so, and was Simpson's right hand. When Simpson told

24

him "hurt," then he hurt someone. When he wa..
"maim," he did that, too—and on the odd occasi..
when Simpson had called upon him to "kill,"—well,
he didn't much like it, but he did it. On the other
hand, he liked hurting and maiming people. He liked
to hear them yell when he broke their bones, and if
they were dead then they couldn't yell any more.

And that was the only reason he didn't like killing
people.

The Nez Perce girl had been named Flower by
Lottie. No one knew what her real name was. The
story went that Lottie had found her when she was
thirteen and had used her to keep house for her in a
couple of her establishments. During that time she
was giving the young girl lessons, so that by the time
she was sixteen she was an accomplished whore—she
just hadn't done any whoring yet. Once the girl had
actually gotten started she turned out to be Lottie's
biggest draw—especially for the past four months
that she had been set up at Bonneville's. Lottie herself
was still a handsome woman, even if she was forty-
four and had some gray streaks in her black hair. She
didn't "perform" any more herself. She always said
that there was nothing worse than an old whore who
didn't know when to quit. Nowadays she just walked
around the place In a lowcut gown, letting the men
ogle her creamy cleavage, content in the knowledge
that she could still give any man in the place more
than he could take.

When Simpson entered Lottie saw him and hurried
to him. Lottie had her eye on Simpson's friend, Al
Nudger. She was eager to find out if Nudger was
"big" all over, but the big man never accompanied
Simpson to her place.

"Where's your friend?" she asked.

"Not today, Lottie," Simpson said.

"When?" she asked. "You been promising to bring him over here sometime, but when?"

Simpson knew that Lottie had her eye on Nudger, and he decided to use that to his advantage.

"I tell you what, Lottie," he said. "You extend me a little credit tonight, and I'll see what I can do about getting Nudge over here—oh, say tomorrow?"

"For a 'little' credit?" she asked, narrowing her eyes. "Why do I get the feeling you just walked into here with empty pockets?"

Simpson contrived to look hurt.

"Empty pockets?" he and. "Would I do that to you, Lottie?"

"Yeah, you would."

"I'm just wondering how bad you really want old Nudge between your sheets."

"Bad enough to give you some credit," she said, "but only for tonight. Which girl you want?"

"The squaw."

"Flower?" she said. "That figures. Give you some credit and you want to tie up my best girl."

"Believe me, Lottie," Simpson said, "tying that gal up is the last thing I have on my mind."

Simpson had Flower's taut little bottom in both of his hands, and she had both muscular thighs wrapped around his middle. Now he knew that she was a whore, and as such she could make a man *think* that he was the best in bed, and that she *knew* how to fake it, but he also knew that she wasn't faking it with him. He was plowing her good and she was moaning and crying in his ear, and he *knew* she wasn't faking, because women—whores or not—just didn't fake it with Derek Simpson.

They didn't have to.

As far as Simpson was concerned, he was God's gift to all women, and he was kind enough to share

26

that gift with as many women as he could.

Simpson pressed Flower down hard into the bed, enjoying the way her hard nipples felt on his chest. He was taking her the way a bull takes its mate, and when he exploded inside of her he bellowed like a bull.

Flower thought that he smelled like a bull, too.

Simpson watched as Flower stood up and began to clean herself in a basin of water. After she was done she put on her dress and started for the door.

"Whoa there, little girl," he said.

The eighteen year old Nez Perce woman turned and looked at him.

"You paid for all night?" she asked.

Simpson decided not to tell her that he hadn't paid for *anything*. It might hurt her feelings if she knew, and he wanted her happy and talkative.

"Sweetheart, do you think you could handle ol' Derek all night?" he asked.

Flower was barely five-two, and if she weighed a hundred pounds it was a lot. She gave the man the answer she knew he wanted.

"No, Mr. Simpson," she said, "probably not."

Flower spoke excellent English. It was something else she had learned from Lottie.

"Come and sit down and rest a minute, Flower."

"I have to go back to work—"

Simpson took out his last dollar and showed it to her.

"What's that for?" she asked.

"Some talk," he said, laying the dollar on the bed, "just between you and me. Lottie doesn't have to know a thing about it."

Flower walked over to the bed and snatched up the dollar, before he changed his mind. It wasn't often she got any money for herself. Lottie treated her good, fed her, clothed her, but she never gave her any money for herself. Every once in a while a man gave her some, but never before had it been to talk.

"What do you want to talk about?" she asked.

"Your people," he said, patting the bed next to him. "Sit down and talk to me about the Nez Perce . . ."

Chapter Three

The next morning Pike was half dressed when Sandy Jacoby walked in.

"What do you think you're doing?" she demanded. She planted her hands on her hips and two spots of red appeared on her cheeks—and she wasn't blushing.

Pike had felt certain that he'd be able to fend her off if she caught him, but now he wasn't so sure. She seemed genuinely angry.

He decided to try and brazen it out.

"I'm leaving," he said. "I feel fine."

"You are not leaving," she said, "and you are far from fine."

"Sandy," Pike said, "I can't stay in this bed another minute—unless, of course, you'd care to get into it with me."

The last had come to him in a flash. He was half kidding, and half hoping that he would scare her into letting him go.

He had done neither.

She was studying him with a contemplative look on her face, and he wondered what was going on inside her pretty head.

"Sandy—"

"I'm thinking," she said, cutting him off. "You mean that if I go to bed with you, you'll stay here for a few more days."

29

"I didn't say a few more days," he said, not even sure they were discussing the matter seriously. "Um, I think I could give it one more day."

"That's not good enough," she said. "If I'm going to give myself to you, I've got to get more than that in return."

"But you will," he said.

"No," she said, "I *know* I'd get that, but I need more than 'I think', and I need more than one more day. I want you to stay off your feet for two more days."

"Wait a minute," he said, waving his hand, "are we seriously discussing —"

"Yes, we are," she said, and she wasn't blushing. She turned around and locked the door, as if to prove that she was totally serious. "I will go to bed with you — make love with — you — if you agree to stay in bed for two more days."

Pike studied her and suddenly, as if to bring her point across even further, she began to unbutton her dress.

"Sandy," he stated, "you don't have to —"

"You started this," she said. Her dress was open to her waist and he could see the creamy smoothness of her breasts, and one brown nipple winking at him. "Are you going to back out?"

"Me?" he asked. "Back out? Not a chance. Not if we're really serious, here."

She removed her dress completely, exposing her beautiful breasts and said, "Does this look like I'm not being serious?"

Pike undressed while she watched him, and he had to admit that it made him self-conscious. When he was totally naked she approached him and put her hand on his broad chest.

"You have a beautiful body," she said. "A strong, beautiful body, and it saved your life."

"I'll thank it later," he said, reaching for her.

"No," she said, dancing out of his reach, "I'[...] it now."

With that she fell to her knees and took his swelling cock in her hands. She rubbed it and cooed to it, and then licked it, long luxurious licks that drove Pike crazy. He reached for her head and cupped it as she took him into her mouth. Her head began to move back and forth as her lips slid up and down the length of him.

"Jesus—" he said as he felt the rush in his loins and then he ejaculated into her mouth with a loud groan . . .

Later she was atop him, riding his rigid penis while he palmed her smooth, hard breasts, thumbing the nipples. She rode him up and down, licking her lips and moaning, and then as she exploded into a frenzy over him she bit her lip, bringing one small drop of blood forth. He pulled her down to him and kissed it away . . .

Still later Pike was down between Sandy's legs, licking the length of her sweet, sticky slit. Her legs were spread as widely as she could spread them and he explored every inch of her with his tongue, finally centering once again on her moistness. His tongue found her rigid clit and began to lash it back and forth, and in circles. He felt her belly begin to tremble and then she lifted her hips off the bed and cried out for him not to stop. She was bucking so violently that it was all he could do to keep his mouth in contact with her . . .

They lay together in his bed and she said, "Do you keep bargains that you make?"

31

Usually."

She propped herself up on her elbow and looked at him closely.

"What do you mean, usually?"

"Well, I may want to amend this particular bargain," he explained.

"In what way?"

"Well . . . I'll stay here for two more days if you'll join me."

She flushed and said, "I can't do this again, not in the daytime. This was . . . bold, I admit, but . . ."

"At night, then," he said, "when no one is around."

"Pike—"

"I'm your patient," he said, "your *only* patient, and require your attention at night."

"Pike—"

"It will make me sleep better."

"Pike—"

He slid his big hand down over her belly into the downy growth farther below and said, "*You'll* sleep better."

She groaned as he dipped his finger into her and she said, "I can't argue with *that!*"

Today, Derek Simpson was not scowling.

He stared across the table at Brick, Nudger, and Graves, and they waited eagerly to hear the words they wanted to hear.

"I've got a plan," Simpson finally said.

Nudger looked at the others with a look that said, "I told you so."

"What is it?" Graves asked.

"Is there money in it?" Brick asked.

Simpson looked at Phil Brick and said reproachfully, "There's always money in my ideas, Brick, you guys know that."

"Sure, Derek, sure," Nudger said, "these guys

know that."

"There is something different about this though," Simpson said, eyeing all three of them.

"What's that?" Graves asked.

Simpson hoped what he was about to say wouldn't scare any of them away. His plan was going to take all four of them to pull off.

Finally, he said it.

"There's also some work involved."

"I thought you were gonna be out of here by today," Skins McConnell said to Pike. He had come alone this afternoon to visit Pike.

"Well, Sandy didn't think I was in any shape to get out of bed, yet," Pike said.

"*Sandy* didn't think . . . McConnell said. "Weren't you the guy who said he was going to be out of here by this morning?"

"That was before she presented her argument," Pike said.

"Her argument?" McConnell said. "What was her argument?"

"Believe me, Skins," Pike said, "she was very persuasive. Did you bring another bottle?"

That night Sandy locked the door and slid into bed with Pike, pressing her hot, naked body against his.

"I feel badly about this," she said.

"Badly?" he said, in disbelief.

"No," she said. "I don't mean about *this?*" "I mean about using this to keep you here."

"Well, you were probably right," he said. "I probably could use another couple of days bedrest."

"Well," she said, I'm going to release you from our deal."

"Release me?"

33

Yes," she said, running her hand over his chest and down across his belly. "That means if you want to leave this bed right now—" Her hand closed around his semi-erect penis, and her thumb massaged the swollen head "—you can go right ahead."

Pike had no intentions of leaving that bed at that moment, but he knew sure as hell that he was out of there the next morning.

"So this is what fresh air smells like?" Pike said to McConnell the next morning.

He had surprised McConnell by meeting him at the door that morning as Skins was coming to see him.

"I don't get it," McConnell said. "Yesterday you said you'd be in bed another day, and this morning here you are, you're out."

"Well," Pike said, "I can be persuasive sometimes, too."

McConnell gave Pike the same kind of puzzled look he'd given him yesterday, when Pike had talked about Sandy's persuasiveness. If it hadn't been for the fact that he didn't even think Pike and Sandy Jacoby *liked* each other . . .

"You know, this must be what it feels like to get out of prison," Pike said.

Chapter Four

When Pike and McConnell walked into the saloon Pike noticed Simpson right away, sitting in a corner with three other men.

"How long have they been here?" he asked.

"A couple of weeks," McConnell said.

"Any trouble?"

"Not yet."

Pike stared at them a moment longer, said, "The king and his court, huh?"

"Huh?" McConnell said.

"Come on," Pike said, "let's get a drink."

In the mountains the time of day really didn't affect the way men drank. Morals weren't the way they were in civilization. Ten in the morning or ten at night was the same to them.

Pike and McConnell approached the makeshift bar of planks laid across barrels and ordered a beer each. Actually, as bars went in the mountain settlements, this one was almost considered fancy.

Pike was still concerned with Simpson and his gang. Trouble usually broke out wherever Derek Simpson showed up, usually while he and his band of morons were trying to put some kind of money making scheme into play.

"Two weeks, huh?" he said, half to himself.

"What's that?" McConnell asked.

Nothing."

Pike didn't think that Simpson had ever gone two weeks without causing trouble in his life.

He was due.

"What's the matter?" Al Nudger asked Simpson.

"Look who just walked in."

Nudger turned and saw Pike at the bar

"I thought he was still supposed to be off his feet," Graves said.

"I can put him off his feet," Nudger said.

"Ease up, Nudge," Simpson said, even though he would have liked to see that match-up. He had long wondered how Nudger would fare against Pike. Nudger was larger, and probably stronger, but Pike was undoubtedly smarter. Still, when Nudger got into a fight he turned into some kind of animal. Simpson had seen Nudger take on three, four men all pounding on him, and him not feeling a thing, actually *loving* the fight, and laying them all out.

"You think you can take Pike, Nudge?" Graves asked.

"Of course I can," Nudger said. "There ain't a man who could stand up to me, am I right, Derek?"

"Dead right, Nudge," Simpson said, "but lay off Pike, all right? At least until I say so."

"I just don't like him, Derek," Nudger said, glaring at Pike's broad back.

"I know, Nudge," Simpson said, "I don't, either, but we got a plan to concentrate on, right?"

"A money-making plan," Nudger said, looking away from Pike now.

"Even if there is some work involved," Ed Graves said.

"A little work ain't gonna kill us," Simpson told them. "Haven't any of you ever done a day's work before?"

36

"Not for a long time," Graves said.

"Not if I can help it," Phil Brick said.

"Well, after *this* day's work we'll be able to sit back a relax for a while," Simpson said.

"I don't even know anything about the Nez Perce Indians, Derek," Phil Graves said.

"Don't worry," Simpson said, "I know all we need to know. This is gonna work, men."

"Sure, Derek," Nudger said. Slowly, his eyes drifted to Pike's back again. He'd almost give up the money he stood to make on Simpson's plan for a chance at Pike.

Almost.

Pike was still preoccupied by Simpson, who was still sitting at his table with his three colleagues.

"Pike," McConnell said.

"What?"

"This is the third time I said your name," McConnell said. "What are you thinking about?"

"Not what, Skins," Pike said, "who?"

"The girl?"

"Girl?"

"Sandy."

"Oh, Sandy . . ." Pike said, a smile coming briefly to his face, and then vanishing. "No, it wasn't Sandy I was thinking about, it was Simpson."

"Look, Pike, I know you and Simpson don't like each other, but don't you think you could ignore him while we're here?"

"I don't see how, Skins," Pike said. "He's here, and that means he's got trouble to cause."

"What kind of trouble could he cause here?" McConnell said. He stole a glance over at Simpson and noticed that while Derek Simpson was not looking their way, the big man, Al Nudger, was.

"Besides," McConnell continued, "Nudger seems

to be the one interested in you, not Simpson."

"Nudger's no problem, Skins."

"He looks like he could be a pretty big problem, to me," McConnell said.

"Physically, but that's to be expected," Pike said. "He's got no brains, so I know what kind of trouble he can cause. Simpson, on the other hand, is no dope. He's mean and nasty, and ignorant about a lot of things, but he's not stupid. He's crafty, and dishonest, and he's always looking to make money—dishonestly."

"Well, we know a lot of men like that, Pike," McConnell said. "There's no formal law in the mountains, so a lot of people are looking to make money off somebody else."

"Why are you defending him?" Pike asked.

"I'm not," McConnell said, "I'm just saying he shouldn't take up so much of your time."

Pike drank some beer and then said, "You're right, Skins, I know you're right—"

"Good—"

"—but that doesn't mean I can make myself stop thinking about him."

"Well then go ahead and think about Sandy, why don't you?" McConnell said.

Pike did, for a moment, and smiled again.

"See?" McConnell said. "Isn't that better?"

"Yes, it's better," Pike said, and thought about Simpson again.

At that moment Whiskey Sam and Rocky Victor entered, making noise, as usual. All eyes went to them as they were in the midst of some argument or other, and then everyone went back to what they were doing.

Whiskey Sam and Rocky Victor moved to the bar to join Pike and McConnell.

"You fellas look like you need fresh drinks," Whiskey Sam said, slapping Skins McConnell on the back.

38

"And I suppose you're buying?" Skins McConnell said.

"Of course I am," Sam said, "in honor of our big friend's freedom."

"And because the old fart hit it big in poker last night," Victor said.

"*You* won at poker?" McConnell said.

"And why is that so hard to believe?" Whiskey Sam demanded.

"Because," McConnell said, "I've played poker with you before. You must have found some real easy pickings. Maybe we'll take advantage of that ourselves, hey Pike?"

Again, Pike had been thinking about Simpson and what mischief he might be up to, and had not heard every word—or even every other word.

"What?" he said, distractedly.

"What's the matter with him?" Whiskey Sam asked. "Hey, Pike, I bought you a fresh beer."

"Thanks, Sam," Pike said, closing his hand over the cold mug.

Whiskey Sam looked at McConnell who said, "He saw Simpson."

"Oh," Sam said, "that scallawag's been here as long as we have."

"And he hasn't caused any trouble?" Pike asked.

Sam took a long swallow of beer and then said, "Not yet," wiping his mouth with his sleeve.

"But you expect him to?" Pike said.

"Sure," Sam said, "why else would he be here—why else was Derek Simpson put on this earth but to cause trouble?"

Apparently, Simpson had chosen just that moment to come to the bar for a fresh beer, and he'd heard Whiskey Sam's remark—as had Al Nudger, who was standing right next to him.

"Shut your mouth, old man," Simpson said. "Nobody asked for your opinion."

39

Pike turned to face Simpson and Nudger and said, "I asked him. If you don't like what you're hearing you could always drink some place else."

"There is no place else to drink," Simpson said.

"Exactly," Pike said, "so why don't shut up and go back to your table."

Nudger made a move toward Pike, but Simpson was standing between them and wouldn't budge. Instead, he turned and handed Nudger two beers.

"Let's go back to our table, Nudge."

"But this bastard—"

"Back to the table!" Simpson said, more forcefully. He turned to pick up the other two beers, looked at Pike, and then turned and followed Nudger.

"Oh yeah," Pike said, "he's planning something."

"Why do you say that?" Sam asked.

"He backed off," Pike said. "He'd never back off unless he had some plans he didn't want spoiled. He's got something planned, and it's going to happen soon."

"Pike," Sam said, "your beer is getting warm." Pike picked up the beer and drained it, then leaned his elbows on the bar and thought more about Derek Simpson.

"Why didn't you let me—" Nudger started.

"We have plans to discuss," Simpson said, "and then we have plans to put into play. We don't need to attract Pike's attention."

"I don't like backing off, Simpson," Nudger said. "I don't want him to think I'm afraid of him."

"He doesn't," Simpson said. "He's not that foolish."

"Oh, yeah? Then what *is* he going to think?" Nudger demanded.

That was when Simpson realized that he had made a mistake.

40

"Damn."

"What is it?" Nudger asked.

"Keep quiet for a minute," Simpson said. "Drink your beer."

By backing away from Pike—by doing something unusual—all he had done was exactly what he *didn't* want to do, attract the man's attention. By acting in a manner not expected of him, he had probably confirmed what Pike was thinking, that he had a plan.

How was he going to put the plan into effect with Pike watching him?

Suddenly, he grinned to himself.

What he was going to have to do now was give Pike something else to think about, besides him.

"Nudger . . ." Simpson said.

"Yeah?" Nudger grumbled.

"I've got a job for you," Simpson said, "and I think you're going to like it."

"I think we've got something to worry about now," Pike said to McConnell.

McConnell looked away from Whiskey Sam and Rocky Victor, who were arguing again, and said, "Why do you say that?"

"Look at Nudger."

McConnell looked across the room at Al Nudger and shuddered.

"He's smiling."

"Exactly."

Chapter Five

"Are you feeling all right?" Sandy asked Pike later that night.

They were in a different bed now — Sandy's bed, in the small shack she lived in behind the larger one they were using as a sort of field hospital.

"Why do you ask that?" Pike said. "I feel fine."

"You seem . . . far away."

"Preoccupied?"

"Yes, that's the word."

"Well, I am," he said. He hugged her to him and said, "I'm sorry . . . I've just got something on my mind."

"What?"

"You wouldn't be interested."

"Of course I would."

He held her in the dark for a few moments and then told her about Simpson, and Nudger, and the others.

"Why do you have to worry about them?" she asked. "You're not the law."

"No, I'm not," Pike said, "but I don't like Simpson and his bunch. If they're out to cause trouble, I'd like to stop them."

"Why?"

Pike didn't think it would be so hard to understand, but maybe it was. Maybe it just seemed to her

like he couldn't mind his own business — ma
was right.

"I guess I'm just nosy," he said, finally.

"That can't be it," she said. "Maybe you're just a good man who doesn't like to see others taken advantage of by bad men."

"Bad men?" Pike repeated. The phrase, though it might have accurately described Simpson and Nudger and the others, seemed . . . naive.

"Isn't that what they are?"

"I suppose so," Pike said, "but I don't know that I'm such a good one."

"Oh, you are," she said, "I can tell you are."

"Just from this?" he asked, sliding his hand over her taut buttocks.

"No," she said, sliding her hand down between his legs to play with him, "not just by this. We don't just do this, we talk."

"What do you want to do now," he said, tracing the crease between her buttocks with his finger, "talk or . . . this?"

She closed her hand around him and said huskily, "What do you think?"

She moved down so that she could use her tongue on him and he relaxed and stopped thinking about Simpson, and Nudger, and — as she took him into her mouth — about *anything* else.

Whiskey Sam and Rocky Victor were arguing. There was nothing unusual about that, they argued all the time — about anything. Observers thought that if the two ever weren't arguing they would have nothing to say to each other — or they'd both be dead.

They were arguing now, as they walked back to their tent, about how long it would take Pike to dispose of Al Nudger in a fight.

"Ten minutes, tops," Whiskey Sam said.

43

Ha!" Rocky Victor said. "You're either overestimating Pike or underestimating Nudger. Don't forget, Nudger is the bigger man—and probably meaner."

"Then why don't you take Nudger?" Whiskey Sam said. "We could bet on the fight?"

"If I was going to bet on the winner, I wouldn't take Nudger, but I am willing to bet on the length of the fight. I think the two of them would go at it for a half an hour at least, before Pike would finish him off."

"Ten minutes," Sam said, shaking his head stubbornly, "at the most."

"Half an hour," Victor said as they approached their tent.

They were so intent on their argument that they didn't see the big man who stepped out from behind their tent.

"Ten minutes—"

"Half hour—"

"You're both wrong!" Al Nudger said.

Both men turned and when they saw Nudger they knew he wasn't there just to solve their argument.

"What do you want?" Whiskey Sam demanded.

"Sam—" Victor said, warningly, but Nudger moved forward and punched Victor in the face. The older man fell over backward and lay still.

"What the—" Whiskey Sam said. He threw a punch at Nudger, which hit the larger man in the chest with no effect.

Nudger laughed and hit Sam in the stomach. Sam doubled over, holding his belly and Nudger took him by the collar and lifted him off the ground effortlessly.

"Old man," he said, "this is going to be a pleasure."

"Put me down and fight like a man," Whiskey Sam growled.

"I'll put you down," Nudger said. He opened his hand so that Sam dropped toward the ground, and

44

then brought his foot up, kicking the slight man before he could land. When he did land he folded himself up in a fetal position, anticipating more kicks. When they came, his protective position did nothing to minimize their force. Nudger kept kicking until he was winded. Without bothering to check on the man's condition, he walked to where the other man was lying and kicked him in the head once, very hard, and then walked away, leaving both of them lying there to be found sometime the next morning.

Part Two

The Plan

Chapter Six

"Who found them?" Pike asked.

"I did," McConnell said.

Pike was back in the room in which he had awakened, only now it was Whiskey Sam and Rocky Victor who were in bed, injured.

"How are they, Sandy?" Pike asked.

"Mr. Victor has a concussion," she said. "He looks as if he was kicked pretty hard in the head."

"What can you do for him?" Pike asked.

"All we can do is wait for him to wake up. If he does, he'll be all right."

Pike looked from Rocky Victor's bed to Whiskey Sam's.

"And Sam?"

"Well," Sandy said, "he is in worse shape. He was apparently kicked repeatedly, in the head and the body. He has a broken arm, probably some broken ribs as well as a concussion."

"What can you do for him?"

"Well, I've set the broken arm—it was broken in two places. I'm hopeful that it will heal properly."

"And if it doesn't?"

"He might not have the use of it."

"And what else?"

"There's nothing I can do for the broken ribs. They have to heal themselves. There was no bleeding from the ath, and I'm hoping that there is no internal bleeding. there is . . ." She left the rest unsaid. "There's also some frostbite, since they were lying out there all night, and when they awake they might have colds . . . or worse."

"So it's the same as with Rocky, huh?" Pike asked. "We just have to wait?"

"I'm afraid so."

Pike looked at McConnell and said, "Let's get out of here."

"Right."

"Sandy, we'll check back later," Pike said.

She moved toward Pike and touched his arm.

"I'm sorry about your friends, Pike," she said. "I'll do all I can."

"I know you will."

When they got outside Skins McConnell said, "They need a real doctor."

"I know," Pike said, "but where are we going to find one?"

"Not on this mountain, that's for sure," McConnell said. "Maybe I should go and look for one, maybe in some town in the valley — "

"By the time you got back here they'd either be dead or out of danger," Pike said. "We'll just have to hope Sandy can help them."

McConnell nodded, and they started to walk.

"Who the hell would do this to them?" McConnell asked.

"I don't know," Pike said. "Was anything taken from them?"

"Well, they still had their rifles and pistols, and their knives. I don't know how much money they had, but Sam looked like he still had most of his winnings on him."

"Then they weren't robbed," Pike said, "they were just . . . beaten."

"For no reason?" McConnell said.

"There has to be a reason, Skins," Pike said. "There *has* to be!"

* * *

"Have you heard anything yet?" Simpson Nudger.

"No," Nudger said.

"How bad did you work on them?" Simpson asked. "Were they dead?"

"I didn't check, Derek," Nudger said.

They were in a tent that the two of them shared, while Graves and Brick shared another.

"Well," Simpson said, "we'll know soon enough. Word will get around."

"I don't think they'll be talking for a while," Nudger said.

"All we need is half the day," Simpson said. "By then we'll be out of here."

"We gonna take those Nez Perce horses today?"

"Tonight," Simpson said.

"How many?"

"Forty head," Simpson said, "and all prime stock. We'll get a high price for them, Nudger, a high price."

"Those Nez Perce will be mad, Derek."

"Sure they will, but they'll come here first."

"Maybe mad enough to wipe this place out?" Nudger suggested.

"Maybe," Simpson said, "but I ain't gonna worry about what happens here after we're gone. Besides, if those two old men die, you'll be wanted for murder."

"Murder?" Nudger said. "Who's gonna know it was me did it if they're dead?"

"Who do you suppose Pike is gonna think did it?" Simpson asked.

Nudger thought a moment then surprised Simpson by saying, "You *and* me."

Simpson stared at Nudger and said, "You know, you're right."

"I am?"

"Maybe we'd better clear out before this afternoon just

se Pike comes looking for us."

He can't prove nothing."

"I know that," Simpson said, "and he might not even think about us, but if he does, I want to be gone."

"You're not afraid of him, are you?"

Simpson turned and gave Nudger a cold look.

"I'm afraid he might ruin our plans, Nudge," Simpson said, "but I ain't afraid of *no* man. You of all people should know that."

Nudger felt ashamed for having suggested it and started to apologize.

"Never mind," Simpson said. "Wake the others and start getting our horses ready. We'll move out as soon as we're outfitted."

"All right, Derek," Nudger said.

As Nudger left, Simpson rubbed his hands together. Forty head of Indian ponies would bring them a mighty fine price, and it would be a while before the Nez Perce discovered that their horses weren't at Bonneville's Fort — if they even bothered trying to find that out before burning the whole place to the ground!

Pike and McConnell found a fire where breakfast could be had and accepted a couple of bowls of mush, and a couple of cups of coffee, both of which were scalding hot. After that they found a couple of rocks to sit on and had their breakfast.

"Sam rubs a lot of people the wrong way, Pike," McConnell said.

"I know."

"I mean, we're his friends and we understand him, but somebody who don't—"

"I know, I know," Pike said, "but who would give him that kind of beating just because he annoyed them?"

"I don't know."

Pike set aside his empty bowl and sipped his coffee. Suddenly, he remembered the altercation last night with

Simpson and Nudger.

"Naw," he said.

"What?"

"Remember last night, when Sam was bad mouthing Simpson?"

"And Simpson came along?"

Pike nodded.

"You think Simpson gave Sam that beating because of what Sam said? But what about Rocky? He didn't say a word."

"He was with him," Pike said. "They were together and there wasn't any way to separate them."

"There usually isn't," McConnell said, "but I don't see this as Simpson's style."

"I do," Pike said, "if you consider that he wouldn't administer the beating himself."

"You mean Nudger?"

"He enjoys that kind of work," Pike said.

"That's not work for him," McConnell said, "that's play."

"Yeah."

They sat quietly for a moment and then McConnell said, "We can't prove it."

"If we could, I wouldn't be sitting here," Pike said. "So what do we do?"

"We wait," Pike said. "When Sam or Rocky wake up they'll tell us who it was."

"And when is that gonna be?"

Pike shook his head heedlessly and said, "I don't know."

"I mean, by the time they wake up, whoever did beat them up might be long gone."

Pike looked at his friend and said, "You have a point. Come on."

Pike stood up and McConnell followed.

"Where are we going?"

"Maybe we can't prove that Nudger and Simpson did it, but that doesn't mean we can't talk to them, does it?"

Chapter Seven

Pike and McConnell checked the grounds of Bonneville's Fort thoroughly, but they could find no sign of Derek Simpson, or his friends.

"What does this mean?" McConnell asked. "That they did it and ran?"

"Not without a good reason," Pike said.

"A good reason for doing it?"

"And a good reason for running."

"Why don't we talk to Kenyon?"

"Good idea."

Jean-Luc Kenyon was the "booshway" of Bonneville's Fort. He was the first man to settle there, and Bonneville's sort of sprang up around him.

Pike hadn't seen Kenyon since his arrival, and he wished they were meeting again under more pleasant circumstances. Pike liked Kenyon. He was one of the few honest men Pike had ever known. Kenyon spoke his mind and the consequences be damned.

They walked to Kenyon's house, a two room shack he had built with his own hands. His woman, a Nez Perce woman, was in front as they approached.

As long as Pike had known Kenyon—about ten years—Black Wing had been his woman. For that same period of time, she had never spoken a word to anyone but Kenyon.

"Is Kenyon here, Black Wing?" Pike asked.

She nodded, and then turned and went into th— with an armload of wood.

"Have you ever heard her speak?" McConnell asked Pike idly.

"Only to Kenyon."

McConnell looked surprised.

"I've never heard her speak, period. Can she speak English?"

"I don't know if she can speak it," Pike said, "but I know she can understand it."

The door to the shack opened and Kenyon stepped out. By any description, Kenyon was an impressive figure of a man. He had the fullest beard Pike had ever seen, and it cascaded down over a paunch that Pike knew was as hard as a stone. Kenyon stood six-feet, but he looked shorter than that because of his girth. At fifty he was still a formidable man in a fight. Pike knew how formidable Kenyon was because they had met by fighting each other. After learning respect for each other they became good friends.

"Pike," Kenyon said. He came down the steps and extended his hand, which Pike accepted. "It's good to see you up and about. I'm sorry I wasn't able to come and see you—"

"Forget that, Jean-Luc," Pike said. "We have something to talk to you about."

"Well, come inside and I'll have Black Wing make some coffee."

"Thanks."

Kenyon shook hands with McConnell and the three of them went inside.

They sat at a handmade wooden table and Black Wing put coffee in front of them, having anticipated her husband's wishes.

"That's what makes her a good wife," Kenyon said, pouring coffee for the three of them.

"Now," he said, "what's wrong?"

Pike told Kenyon about Whiskey Sam and Rocky Vic-

being attacked and injured. He explained the extent of
their injuries, and Kenyon listened intently.

"I'm sorry to hear about this," Kenyon said. "Who did
it?"

"We don't know yet," Pike said. "Neither man is awake
to tell us."

"But we have our suspicions," McConnell said.

"And they are?"

"Simpson and his bunch," Pike said.

Kenyon made a face.

"I knew Simpson was trouble when he arrived, but I
had no call to ask him to leave."

"We understand that."

"You don't know for sure that he did it?"

"No," Pike admitted. "We had an altercation with him
last night, him *and* Nudger," Pike said, and explained
what had happened.

"Do you think that was sufficient provocation for
Simpson to send Nudger after Sam and Rocky?"

"I wouldn't think so, ordinarily," Pike said, "but today
we went looking for Simpson and Nudger and the
others—er, just to talk to them . . ."

"Of course," Kenyon said. "What did they have to say
for themselves?"

"They're not here," McConnell said. "They've apparently left."

"Run off after doing the deed," Kenyon said. "Is that
what you think?"

"It's a possibility," Pike said. "It's also a possibility that
Simpson had Sam and Rocky beaten up as a diversion."

"A diversion?" Kenyon said. "From what?"

"I wish I knew." Pike said. "Knowing Simpson, he has
something planned, and maybe he wanted to divert my
attention from him."

"If that was his plan," Kenyon said, "it would seem he's
done just the opposite."

"Right," Pike said "Jean-Luc, I'd like to find out what
Simpson's up to."

56

"How can I help?"

"Ask around," Pike said. they won't tell me. Maybe she will tell you things they won't tell me. Maybe — a bartender, a whore — heard something. Maybe they don't know what it means, but we will."

"I'll pass the word around," Kenyon said. "Will you keep me posted on Sam and Rocky's condition? If one of them wakes up and confirms what you suspect, I'll put together a posse and we'll go after Simpson and his bunch."

"A posse?" Pike asked.

"What passes for a posse, then," Kenyon said. "I know we have no law up here, but that doesn't mean that Simpson and his kind can do what they like without paying the consequences."

"All right," Pike said. He and McConnell stood up and prepared to leave.

Kenyon stood and said, "We won't let this pass, Pike. I promise you."

"I knew you'd feel that way, Jean-Luc. Thanks — and thanks for the coffee. Thank Black Wing for us."

"I will."

McConnell and Pike left Kenyon's home and stopped outside.

"Well," McConnell said, "with Kenyon passing the word, maybe we'll know something soon."

"I hope so," Pike said. "I don't think I'm going to be able to just sit around for very long. That stay in bed has given me the itch to move on."

"We're not moving on until we find out —"

"No," Pike said, "we'll resolve this before we move on. That's for sure."

They stopped in to see if Whiskey Sam or Rocky Victor had awakened yet, or if their conditions had changed.

"No change, I'm afraid," Sandy said.

"But they haven't gotten any worse, have they?" Pike

57

ked.

"No," she said, "no had waited for him outside, worse."

Pike nodded. McCo

and he turned to lead it yet?" Sandy asked.

"Do you know w said, "No . . . not for sure, but I

Pike turned back ea."

have a petty good

"Whe you know for sure, you're going after them, aren't you?"

Pike stared at her.

"Kenyon will put together a posse and yes, I will ride with them."

"But you won't just go as a member of the posse," she said. "This is personal for you."

Pike pointed to the two beds and said, "Those two men are friends of mine." He didn't say any more. In his mind, that explained it all as well as possible.

She closed her hand around his forearm and said, "I know."

Outside McConnell said, "Any change?"

"None," Pike said, "none for the better, or for the worse."

"Well, I guess that's something."

"I tell you what," Pike said.

"What?"

"Why wait for Kenyon to put the word out? Let's start asking some questions ourselves."

"I'm for that."

"Let's split up," Pike said. "We'll meet later for a beer and compare notes. After that, we can check in with Kenyon and see what he's found out."

"Let's do it, then," McConnell said.

"We'll meet in three hours."

McConnell said, "We should be good and thirsty by then."

Chapter Eight

Pike decided to check out Lottie McCullers's whorehouse—and it was a house. The two story wooden structure was the largest building at Bonneville's Fort, and as such stood out boldly. For this reason Lottie did not even have a sign telling people what the building was. Everyone *knew*.

Asking around, Pike discovered that Lottie McCullers had come to town with four girls and, apparently, enough money to hire enough men to build her a building that could have been used as a hotel—and probably would, someday.

Pike went to Lottie's and found that it was not yet open for business. He knocked on the front door, waited, and then *pounded* on it. Finally, someone opened it.

"What?"

He saw one blue eye glaring up at him tiredly. The other eye was hidden beneath a lock of blond hair. The woman had a wrap held closely around her, but judging from the eye he could see, and the hand holding the wrap together, she was in her thirties. The hand wasn't soft any more, but it didn't have the loose-skinned look of an old woman's hand. The eye was clear—though bleary—and had some lines around it, but not so many that she could be more than thirty-five.

"I'd like to see Lottie."

"She's asleep."

"Wake her up."

The eye widened at the idea.

"I can't do that."

"Then let me in and I'll do it."

The eye widened even more.

"I can't do that, either."

"Well, what can you do?"

In answer to that question she tried slamming the door in his face, but that didn't work. Pike had time to get his big foot in the way.

"No," he said to her, "you can't do that, either." He pushed the door open and she was unable to resist his strength. She stepped back and he entered and closed the door behind him. The woman had lost hold of her wrap and Pike was able to see her plump body, pale and soft. She had pushed her hair back and he saw that her face was also becomingly plump, pretty but with the hint of a double chin forming. He had been right. She was about thirty-five, and had maybe five good years left in her.

"Now you can tell her I forced my way in," he said. "Go and wake her."

"I told you I can't—" the woman started, but another woman's voice cut her off.

"It's all right, Giselle," the woman said. "I'm already awake."

Pike looked at the woman standing on the steps. She had dark hair, streaked with gray, and the robe she wore was worth a hundred of the wrap the other woman was wearing. It was closed, but that didn't hide the fact that the woman was full bodied and handsome. She was probably ten years older than Giselle, but she had taken much better care of herself. She had been smart enough to move into the management area of the business.

"Go back to your room, Giselle."

Giselle nodded and went up the stairs, woman Pike assumed was Lottie McCullers.

"Miss McCullers?"

"That's me," she said, coming down the rest of the way. "Who are you?"

"My name's Pike."

"Should that mean something to me?"

"I don't think so."

"Then why have you pushed your way in here?"

"I'm sorry about that," he said. "I was trying to give the other girl — Giselle — no choice, so that you wouldn't be able to blame her."

"Oh," Lottie said, "a gentleman."

"No, Ma'am."

"Well, now that you're in, come into the sitting room and tell me what I can do for you."

He followed her into the sitting room, inhaling the perfume she was trailing behind her.

"You're not here for a girl, I assume," Lottie said, seating herself. "Please, sit down."

Pike sat and said, "Actually, I am here for a girl, but I want to talk to them."

"Even if all you want to do is talk," Lottie said, "you'll have to wait until we're open and pay your money like anyone else."

"I don't have time."

"What's your hurry?"

"Do you know a man named Simpson?"

"I know every man in Bonneville's Fort, Mr. Pike — which means you've just recently arrived."

"That's right," Pike said.

"What's your interest in Simpson?"

"He's a troublemaker."

"Tell me something I don't already know."

"I believe he had two of my friends beaten up so badly that they haven't waked up yet."

"I'm sorry."

"Simpson's left the settlement, and I believe he's on

61

way to cause some kind of trouble."

"How can I help you?"

"I'd like to talk to whatever girls he . . . frequented."

She laughed and said, "You could have said 'used,' Mr. Pike. I would not have been offended. Simpson used all of my girls at one time or another."

"I need to know if he talked to them about anything."

"He wasn't the talkative type. He usually did what he had to do and left — except — "

"Except when?"

"Well," she said, "the other night he did spend a little more time with one of my girls than usual."

"Which one?"

"An Indian girl I have," she said. "Her name is Flower."

"Can I talk to her?"

Lottie studied Pike for a few moments, and then said, "It'll cost you. I'll have to wake her, and she needs her beauty sleep."

"I'll pay."

She studied him again and then shrugged her shoulders.

"All right," she said, "I'll get her. Wait here, please."

"I appreciate this."

"Never mind your appreciation," she said, "just have your money ready."

"What kind of Indian is she?" Pike asked.

She stopped just short of the doorway and said, "Nez Perce."

While waiting, Pike counted out his money and hoped he had enough to satisfy Lottie McCullers. After about ten minutes he heard footsteps on the stairs, and then Lottie McCullers entered, with

62

Flower behind her.

Flower was a small girl, young and very pretty. had the blackest hair Pike had ever seen, worn long and parted in the center. She was completely covered from head to toe in a robe, and she seemed to glide as she crossed the room. Pike was willing to bet that Flower did very well for Lottie.

"I'll have to stay in the room with you," Lottie McCullers said.

"That's no problem," Pike said. "Does she speak English?"

"Yes," Lottie said. "You can speak directly to her."

"Flower," he said, "do you know a man named Simpson?"

"Yes."

"He spent sometime with you the other night, didn't he?"

"Yes."

"What did you do?"

"We had sex."

"Did you do anything else?"

Pike saw Flower look toward Lottie.

"No."

"Are you sure, Flower?"

"I am sure."

Pike studied the girl for a moment, and then looked at Lottie.

"She's lying."

"How do you know?"

"She's afraid to say something in front of you."

Lottie looked at Flower.

"Is that true, Flower?"

The young girl didn't answer. Lottie went over and stood by the chair the girl was sitting in and stroked her hair.

"Flower, you don't have to be afraid to speak in front of me," Lottie said, soothingly. "You know that."

63

Flower hunched her shoulders, as if she thought Lottie was going to hit her.

"What would she be afraid to talk about in front of you?" Pike asked.

Lottie thought a moment, then smiled and said, "Money." Addressing herself to Flower Lottie said, "Is this about money?"

Flower hesitated, then she nodded.

"Did Simpson give you money that you did not give to me?"

Flower closed her eyes and nodded.

"How much?" Lottie asked.

Flower hesitated a long time, and Lottie gave her as much time as she needed. Pike was impressed with the way the older woman was handling the situation.

"A dollar."

Lottie laughed and said, "A dollar?"

"Yes."

"Oh, honey," Lottie said, "you can keep the dollar. Just tell the man what he wants to know."

Flower raised her head and looked at Pike.

"We talked."

"About what?"

"About my people."

"The Nez Perce?"

"Yes."

"What did he want to know?"

"He wanted to know all about my people, and how they feel about their horses."

"Horses?"

"Yes," she said, "he asked what they would do if someone stole their horses from them."

Pike knew what the Nez Perce would do. They would go and get their horses back . . . if they knew who had taken them.

"What else, Flower?"

"That is all."

"Did he tell you why he wanted to know all of

this?" Pike asked.

"No."

Pike sat back in his chair and stroked his mustache thoughtfully. He didn't like what he was thinking at the moment.

"Is that what you wanted to know?" Lottie McCullers asked.

"Yes, that's it, that's all," Pike said. "Thank you, Lottie."

Lottie touched the girl gently on the shoulders with both hands and said, "You can go back to your room now, Flower."

The young girl stood up and left the room. Pike stood up and started to hand Lottie what he hoped was enough money. She intercepted his hand and closed it.

"You know what this means?" she asked.

"I have an idea."

"So do I," she said. "Keep your money and stop that sonofabitch before he does something we'll all have to pay for."

Pike surprised himself by leaning over and kissing Lottie's scented cheek.

"Thanks, Lottie."

Chapter Nine

"He's gonna what?" McConnell asked.

"He's going to steal horses from the Nez Perce," Pike said.

They each had a beer and as soon as they sat down Pike told McConnell what he believed.

"Where did you find this out?"

"From a Nez Perce whore," Pike said.

"Simpson *told* her he was going to steal horses — " McConnell said.

"No, he didn't tell her," Pike said, "but he asked her all kinds of questions about her people, about how they would react to having horses stolen from them. Don't you see? That's his plan, to steal horses from the Nez Perce and then to sell them."

"Pike . . . would Simpson be that stupid?"

"I don't know that it is stupid," Pike said.

"To steal horses from the Nez Perce?" McConnell said. "They'll hunt him and the others down like dogs."

"If they know he did it."

"Who else — "

"What if the Nez Perce come here?" Pike asked. "What if they think someone from *here* did it?"

"If what you're saying is so, they'd be right. Someone from here will do it."

"Yes, but when they come here Simpson and his

66

men will be gone."

"So we—or Kenyon—just tells the Nez Perce did it."

"If you were an Indian would you believe that one white man would give up another white man . . . to Indians?"

"We're not as loyal to each other as the Indians are," McConnell said.

"Would the Indians know that?"

"Look, if what you're saying is so, we've got to tell Kenyon."

Pike stared at his friend.

"You're not totally convinced about this, are you?"

McConnell made a face and said, "No, I'm not."

"Then how the hell are we going to convince Kenyon?" Pike said. "And by the time we do convince him, and he puts together some kind of a posse, Simpson and his men will be long gone."

"Then what are you suggesting?" McConnell said.

Pike opened his mouth to answer and McConnell stopped him. "Wait a minute. I know what you're suggesting."

"What?"

"That we go out and stop Simpson ourselves." Pike nodded and said, "Before it gets to the point where we have to convince the Nez Perce that their horses are not here."

"Just the two of us?" McConnell asked.

"Who would go with us?"

McConnell thought a moment and then said, "The only two men I know would go with us are laid up."

"Right," Pike said, "Sam and Rocky. We're going to have to do this ourselves, Skins."

McConnell stared into his beer mug.

"We should talk to Kenyon," McConnell said.

Pike hesitated a moment and then said, "All right, let's talk to him, but if he's not ready to act immediately, then we will. Agreed?"

"Agreed."

Kenyon listened patiently to what Pike had to say, but Pike could tell from the look on the man's face that he wasn't convinced.

"I don't know . . ." Kenyon said. "You're basing this on the word of a Nez Perce whore."

"Why else would Simpson ask her so many questions about her people?"

"I don't know," Kenyon said, "but to draw the conclusion you have . . ." Kenyon looked at McConnell and said, "What about you, Skins. Do you go along with this?"

"It's one way to figure it," McConnell said, evasively.

"Yes, but are you convinced that Pike is reading it right?"

McConnell hesitated and Pike saved him the trouble of answering.

"No, he's not convinced," Pike said, "but he's willing to go along with me."

"Well, Pike," Kenyon said, "in my position I have to be able to do more than just go along with you. I have to be able to believe, without a doubt, that I'm doing the right thing."

"Jean-Luc," Pike said, "when's the last time you knew that, without a doubt?"

Pike didn't wait for an answer. He turned and walked out.

McConnell shrugged at Kenyon, who said, "I'm sorry." McConnell nodded and followed Pike out.

Outside Pike said, "Well?"

"Well what?"

"Are you still willing to go along?"

"Sure," McConnell said.

"Why?"

"Because even if you're wrong about the horses,"

McConnell said, "I still think it was Simp... had Sam and Rocky beaten up. For that reason ... I'm willing to go after them."

"There's two of us and four of them," Pike said, reminding his friend.

"Yeah," McConnell said, "they're outnumbered, ain't they?"

Pike grinned and slapped his friend on the back.

"Hey, you haven't told me what you found out, yet," he said, then.

"Not much," McConnell said. "Only that Simpson and the others seem to have left early today, probably just before we started looking for them."

"That means they haven't got that much of a head start," Pike said. "They shouldn't be too difficult to track."

"Pike, if they are going to steal horses from the Nez Perce, they must know where those horses are."

"Right," Pike said, "so?"

"So, it would help if we knew, also."

"You're right about that," Pike said, "but who would know that?"

"The Nez Perce girl you spoke to at Lottie's?" McConnell suggested.

"No," Pike said, shaking his head, "she wouldn't know. She hasn't lived among them for a long time— and the same goes for Black Wing, Kenyon's woman." Pike shook his head and said, "Kenyon."

"You're disappointed in him."

"Yes."

"Don't be," McConnell said. "This whole place is his responsibility. He can't act on your feelings."

Pike made a face and said, "You're right. Let's get back to the question about the horses. Somebody has to know where they are?"

"Well," McConnell said, "somebody must know where the Nez Perce are. If we find them, maybe we find the horses."

"All right, then," Pike said, "let's start asking around again."

"I'll put together the outfit for the trip," McConnell said. "We leave in the morning?"

"We leave in the morning," Pike said, nodding.

"Uh, where do you intend to spend the night?"

"Where do you think?"

"I'll meet you in front of the trading post," McConnell said. "It'll be closed that early, but I'll have the supplies by then."

"Right," Pike said. "I'll check on Sam and Rocky before we leave."

"No reason to meet again tonight," McConnell said. "Whichever one of us locates the Nez Perce can tell the other in the morning."

"Right," Pike said. "I'll see you then."

McConnell waved and once again they went off in separate directions to ask questions.

Chapter Ten

McConnell found a man named Harry Falk who liked to talk. In fact, he liked to drink and talk, so McConnell gave him ample opportunity to do both.

"Here," McConnell said, putting a fresh beer in front of the man, "drink up."

"Sure, thanks," Harry Falk said. He was a big man gone fat and the remnants of his last meal were floating around in his beard.

"Anyway, like I says, the Nez Perce camp is pretty durn near impossible to get near."

"Why is that?"

"Well, they picked the perfect place to set up, that's why. They're in a basin with one way in and out, and that's guarded every second by two bucks."

McConnell stroked his jaw.

"How could somebody think that it would be easy to get near them?"

"Who'd want to?" Harry Falk asked.

"Never mind," McConnell said, "just tell me. Looking at their setup, could someone mistakenly decide that they'd be easy to hit?"

"Hit for what?"

"Horses, let's say," McConnell said. "Suppose somebody wanted to steal their horses?"

"That'd be crazy?" Falk said. "Who'd want to do such a durn fool thing?"

"Nobody," McConnell said, patiently. He hoped that he hadn't fed the man too much beer. "We're just supposin', here, remember?"

"Well, if we're jest s'posin'," Falk said, "if you don't get down real close you might not realize that they're camped in a basin. It looks flat unless you go down close and see that there's one way in and one way out."

"And you've been down close?"

"Sure have," Falk said. "I done some tradin' with the Nez Perce. Also the Crow, and the Snake—"

"Never mind—"

"You know," Falk went on drunkenly, "the Snake Indians—now their horses could be had—"

"Never mind," McConnell said, again. "Can you tell me where the Nez Perce are?"

"Sure, I could," Falk said, "but I could take you there better."

"Would you?"

"Are you payin'?"

"I could be."

"Then I'll take you."

Falk started to lift his beer and McConnell put his hand on his arm to stop him.

"Are you gonna remember this in the morning?"

"Sure I will," Falk said. "You think I can't hold my beer? 'Scuse me, I gotta go outside and piss."

"Don't forget to come back," McConnell said, "we've got to talk price."

"I'll be back," Falk said.

McConnell watched the big man waddle between the tables and then go out the door to relieve himself. If what Falk was saying was true, and Simpson and his bunch did try for the Nez Perce horses, then the Indians might do their job for them.

Still, they'd have to go out and make sure, anyway.

He hoped Falk wasn't just a fat blowhard, and that he really *did* know where to find the Nez Perce.

72

* * *

Simpson sat and looked off into the darkness. Nudger was on guard, while Brick and Graves sat on the other side of the fire, quietly.

It had been a miscalculation. That was what Simpson had called it and, with Nudger backing him up, the other two had no choice but to accept the explanation.

They had ridden to where Harry Falk had told them the Nez Perce were and had moved in close, so that they were almost close enough to touch the two braves on guard. At the last minute, though, Simpson had noticed that the Nez Perce had made their camp in a shallow basin, and that the two braves on guard were blocking the only way in and out. If they went inside and things didn't go just right, they'd be trapped. On top of that, it looked as if there were more Nez Perce in the camp than he had been told by Harry Falk—and after he paid that fat bastard the last of his money.

"We can't go in," Simpson had said. "Let's go."

"What are you talking about?" Nudger had asked.

"Never mind!" Simpson had hissed. "Let's pull back and I'll explain."

After they had put some distance between themselves and the Nez Perce camp, they had camped and Simpson had explained his "miscalculation."

Brick and Graves reacted badly.

"What?" Graves said. "After we came all the way out here, after the promises you made—"

"Look," Simpson said, "I told you, it was a miscalculation."

"A miscalculation?" Brick asked.

"Yeah," Nudger said, "don't you know what that is?"

"Well . . . sure . . ." Brick said, looking at Graves, who shrugged.

"Look," Simpson said, "this is not a total loss."

"What do you mean?" Graves asked.

"The Snake Indians are camped nearby," Simpson said. "We'll just take their horses, instead."

"The Snake Indians are not Nez Perce," Graves said. "Their horses won't bring the same price—"

"So, who has to know we took the horses from the Snake, and not the Nez Perce?"

"Yeah," Nudger said, Graves and Brick fell silent.

Now, sitting at the fire, Simpson knew that tomorrow they'd have to take the Snake horses, just to reinforce his hold on Brick and Graves. He had the feeling that if Al Nudger hadn't been along, Brick and Graves might even have left him.

Derek Simpson didn't know it—or, if he did, he wouldn't admit it to himself—but without someone to follow him, he'd be nothing.

Tomorrow, he'd restore Brick's and Graves' faith in him—and maybe in himself.

Pike raised himself up off Sandy and looked down at her. His penis was buried deep inside of her, and as he drove into her she bit her lip. Her nostrils flared as she groaned and there was a sheen of sweat on her face. He lowered his head and kissed her lips and tasted her sweat on them.

"Oooh Pike . . ." she groaned, digging her nails into his hard buttocks. He kept one hand on each side of her, taking his weight off her as he continued to move in her, and watched with fascination the gamut of expressions that moved across her face. Finally, the cords on her neck stood out, she bit her lip and closed her eyes tightly and he knew she was going over the edge . . .

"You're leaving in the morning?" she asked him

later.

"Yes," he said. "Any [...] [...] [...]ght be a change by then?"

"It's possible," she sa[...], there [...] voice did not give him a lot of he tone over voice

"If one of them should wa[...]nd say [...]pson's name," he said, "or Nudg[...]"

"You wouldn't have to [...]er them a[...]one," she said, "you and McConne[...]"

"That's right."

She shook her head a[...] up in bed. He saw her reach for her clothes a[...] said, "Where are you going?"

"To check on them[...] said. "I'll be back."

"I'll be here."

She looked down [...], touched his face, and then finished dressing [...] left.

Pike had spoken [...]man named Michaels who had given him a rou[...]ea of where the Nez Perce might be camped. [...] hoped that McConnell had found someone to g[...]them more than just a rough idea.

There had been no change in the condition of Whiskey Sam and [...]cky Victor when Sandy checked during the night, and by morning there still had not been any change. Pike left Sandy asleep and walked to the trading post, where he was supposed to meet McConnell. When he got there he was surprised to see McConnell waiting with another man, and four horses.

"Who's this?" he called out.

He reached the two men and saw that the stranger was not an impressive specimen. He did not seem to be wide awake yet. His eyes were red-rimmed, his beard was dirty, and he didn't look like he'd last very long on the back of a horse. McConnell must have ad a good reading him along.

"This is ... ike," McConnell said.

"Falk."

"I've h ... of ... ike," Falk said, but he didn't go on.

"Why ... Mr ... here, Skins?" Pike asked.

"Mr. F ... says ... nows where the Nez Perce are camped," McCo ... aid. "He says he can take us there."

"For a price," ... "for a price."

"Yes," McConn ... lded.

"Have you and ... k agreed on a price."

"We have."

"I was drunk," F ...

"We agreed on a ... d.

him you wouldn't lik ... McConnell said. "I told morning." ... he tried to raise it in the

"Oh," Pike said, mov ...

towered over, "I don't th ... loser to Falk, whom he that, Skins ... would y ... r. Falk would try to do hand on Falk's shoulder a ... Mr. Falk?" He put his

"No," Falk said gasping ... queezed it hard. wouldn't do that." ... m the pain, "n-no I

Pike removed his hand. H ... aw that McConnell had gotten just enough supplie ... o accommodate one pack animal. He walked to ... s own horse and mounted up.

"Are we ready to go?" he asked.

"We're ready," McConnell said, "aren't we, Falk?"

"Yeah," Falk said, sourly, "we're ready."

Part Three

Black Cherry Joe

Chapter Eleven

Pike quickly found out how wrong he had been about Harry Falk.

Despite his appearance, it seemed that Falk actually could sit a horse, if not with grace, at least with some efficiency. He also seemed to know his way around well enough, red-rimmed eyes or not.

"Actually," he said at one point, "I operate a lot better with a nip or two under my belt."

He proceeded to produce a bottle, from which he took a nip or two and then put it away without offering to share it.

Pike thought the man a pig, but agreed that he knew his way around the mountains.

"Where are we headed?"

"About half a day's ride due west," Falk said.

"That close?" Pike asked. "Half a day?"

"Why not?" Falk asked. "The Nez Perce—at least, this bunch—aren't interested in fighting. They want to be let alone, do some trading—"

"Which you provide them with."

"I have that honor, yes," Falk said. "They trust me."

Although Pike's opinions of the man's prowess might have changed, he still was not quite sure that he would trust him.

"Would you fellas mind telling me why we're out

." Falk asked.

McConnell looked at Pike and Pike gave him a
Why not?" shrug.

"We're trying to prevent someone from giving your
Nez Perce a reason to change their peaceful ways,"
McConnell said.

"How so?" Falk asked.

"If Derek Simpson steals their horses," Pike said,
"they'll have something to fight about."

Falk reined his horse in abruptly and began to
laugh uproariously.

"What's so funny?" Pike demanded.

Falk continued to laugh and it seemed that they
would have to wait until he got it out of his system
before they would get any answers.

Finally, the laughter seemed to die down and Falk
was able to speak.

"You mean that's why Simpson wanted to know
where he could find the Nez Perce?" he asked. "He
wanted to steal their horses?"

Pike and McConnell exchanged a glance.

"You told Simpson where he could find the Nez
Perce?" Pike asked.

"Well, of course."

"Why?"

"He paid me."

"But he didn't say why he wanted to find them?"

"I assumed he wanted to try to trade with them,"
Falk said. "I had no idea he wanted to rustle horses.
That's crazy."

"You don't think it could be done?" Pike asked.

"Oh, it could be done, all right," Falk said, "but
not by four men."

Pike reined his horse in and McConnell and Falk
followed his example.

"What's the matter?" McConnell asked.

"Simpson's no dummy, Skins," Pike said. "When
he gets close to the situation he should be able to tell

80

whether it can be done or not."

"What do you think he'll do?"

"I know what I'd do," Pike said. "I'd pull out, but then he'd have to justify that to the other three men."

"The other two," McConnell said, correcting Pike. "Nudger will back him no matter what."

"You have a point," Pike said.

"So what will he do?"

"He's going to have to try and come up with an alternative plan."

"Like what?" McConnell asked.

"Like stealing someone else's horses." Pike said.

Both Pike and McConnell turned to look at Falk, who had been listening to them, and then McConnell suddenly remembered something Falk had said the night before.

"Falk," he said, "last night you said something about the Snake Indians?"

"I did?" Falk said.

"Yes," McConnell said, trying to jog the man's memory, "we were talking about somebody stealing horses from the Nez Perce . . ."

"I remember," Falk said. "I said that the Snake Indians' horses could be had."

"Would they do that, then?" Pike said. "Would they try to steal horses from the Snake Indians, instead?"

"I would," Falk said. "It would be easier to steal from them than from the Nez Perce."

"Would they go after their horses?"

"Oh, sure," Falk said, "they'd try to get them back just as hard as the Nez Perce would."

"Well, we have a choice then," Pike said. "We can keep going to the Nez Perce camp to check and see if Simpson made a try, or we can assume that he didn't and ride to the Snake camp." He looked at Falk and said, "You *could* find the Snake Indians, couldn't you?"

"Sure."

Something occurred to Pike.

"Did you tell Simpson where they were, as well?" he asked.

"You know, I think I did," Falk said.

"What if we make the wrong decision, Pike?" McConnell asked. "What if we go one way and Simpson goes the other? We could lose him."

"We'll have to split up, then."

"Split up how?" McConnell asked.

Pike only took a second to decide.

"You and Falk keep going to the Nez Perce camp, and I'll find the Snake Indians." He turned to Falk and said, "You'll tell me how to find them."

"I will?" Pike gave Falk a hard look and said, "Oh, sure, I will."

Falk proceeded to give Pike directions to the Snake camp.

"If you get into trouble you're going to be on your own, you know," McConnell told him, as if reading Pike's mind.

"I know that," Pike said. "Look, Skins, don't waste your time worrying about me, okay? Look after yourself."

"And me," Falk said, but neither Pike nor McConnell paid him any mind.

Pike dismounted, went to the packhorse and removed some supplies for himself, including some dried meat. He decided that he could do without coffee for a while.

"Let's plan on meeting up at Bonneville's Fort in two days," Pike said, mounting up again, "unless something goes wrong."

"Let's hope nothing does go wrong," Skins McConnell said.

"Dealing with the Nez Perce and the Snake," Harry Falk said, "don't bet against it."

McConnell gave Falk a look of distaste, "Thanks

for sharing that with us, Falk."

"Look," Simpson said. "Two braves guarding the horses, and that's it."

"How do we get close enough?" Graves asked.

"We'll need a diversion," Simpson said.

"Two of us go for the horses and two of us make up a diversion?" Brick asked.

"No," Simpson said, "one man creates a diversion, and the other three take the horses."

The other three men all looked at each other, and they were all wondering the same thing.

"Who creates the diversion?" Graves finally asked.

"I do," Simpson said. "It's the most important part of the plan, I wouldn't trust it to any of you."

Simpson led the way away from the Snake camp, where he felt he could talk to his men without alerting the Indians to their presence.

"All right, listen up," Simpson said. "We use the same plan I outlined for the Nez Perce horses."

Brick frowned and said, "What was that?"

"I'll go over it again." Simpson was patient. "Just remember that once we commit to this nobody pulls out. If somebody does, and I live through this, that man is dead. Understood?"

They all nodded, though none with enthusiasm.

"All right then, listen . . ."

Chapter Twelve

Pike followed Harry Falk's directions, riding at a leisurely pace. He didn't want to attract any attention. Rushing headlong when you didn't know what you were rushing into was a bad habit to get into, and one that Pike had studiously avoided acquiring.

Pike rode until just before dark and then stopped and dismounted. He knew he should have camped for the night, but he also knew he wasn't that far from where the Snake camp was supposed to be. He decided to walk some, leading his horse, on the off chance that he'd reach the camp before darkness forced him to stop. If he stopped, he'd have to build a fire, and that would alert the Indians that someone was nearby.

Pike thought he heard something. He stopped short and listened intently, but didn't hear anything after that. He *felt* that he was being watched. He waited, and when nothing happened he decided to do the only thing he could think of. He took his rifle and his Kentucky pistol, put them down on the ground, and then walked his horse away from them. He dropped the horse's reins to the ground, and then squatted down on his haunches to wait.

It took about twenty minutes, but they finally came out. There were three of them, and they were definitely Snake. They walked to where Pike had left his weapons, and one of them picked them up. Then another walked to Pike, looked down at him, and said something that Pike couldn't understand. When it became clear that Pike could not understand him the Indians simply waved at Pike to follow. Pike stood up and the Indian relieved him of his knife. When he reached for his horse the Indian stepped between him and the animal and shook his head.

"Whatever you say," Pike said, backing away from the horse. "Lead the way."

With one brave leading his horse, and one carrying his weapons, Pike followed the three of them, presumably—hopefully—to their camp.

"I wonder how Pike is doing?" McConnell said.

"Didn't he tell you to worry about yourself, and not him?" Falk asked.

McConnell looked at Falk and asked, "Do you have any friends?"

"No."

"I could have guessed that."

"Never had no need for friends," Falk said, defensively.

"Yeah, well, don't worry," McConnell said, "from where I stand you don't look like you're in any danger of suddenly finding some."

"What are friends?" Falk asked. "Would Pike loan you money?"

"Yes."

"Would he share a woman with you?"

"Yes."

"Well, would he *die* for you?"

"Yes."

Falk looked stunned for a moment, then repeated glumly, "What good are friends."

"How close are we?" McConnell asked.

"We should be seeing Nez Perce any second now,"

Falk said.

At that point they were suddenly surround by Indians on foot. If they hadn't been talking, McConnell thought, they might have heard them. Since they were on horseback they might have been able to ride down the braves, but McConnell didn't think that was a realistic course of action. At this point he would rather talk to the Nez Perce than be on the run from them.

"Easy," he told Falk. "Don't do anything rash."

He looked at Falk and saw that the man was unnerved by their situation.

"Do you know any of these braves?"

"Why the hell should I know any of them?" Falk demanded nervously.

"Well, you've traded with them," McConnell said, "I figured you might know one or two of them."

"Traded with them?"

McConnell hesitated a moment, then said, "You *have* traded with the Nez Perce, haven't you?"

Falk looked at McConnell and said, "Holy Christ, you didn't really believe all that crap, did you?"

It was after dark when they reached the Snake camp. The braves with Pike's horse and weapons went their own way while the third brave indicated that Pike should follow him farther. Pike did so, and followed him to a teepee. The brave motioned for Pike to enter, and when he did the big man found that he was alone. He turned and saw that the brave had not entered with him. He assumed that he was to wait, and sat down, Indian style.

He wished he had the makings of a fire.

"What do we do?" Falk asked.

"Nothing," McConnell said, "we wait for them to do something."

"Like kill us?"

"If they wanted to kill us, they would have done it by now."

"Let's take 'em," Falk said.

McConnell looked at Falk and said, "Your hands are shaking so bad you'd drop your rifle. Just sit still and don't do anything."

"We're gonna die."

"Falk," McConnell said, "shut up."

McConnell looked around them and counted nine Nez Perce. He couldn't tell by looking at them whether they were mad about something—like maybe losing some horses?—or just curious. So far none of them had made a move, either friendly or aggressive. He counted five who were armed with a rifle, the others had either lances or bows and arrows.

"What are we waitin' for?" Falk hissed.

"We're waiting for them to decide what they want to do with us," McConnell said, "because there's nothing *we* can do with *them* at this point."

Falk was about to say something when one Nez Perce brave started moving toward them.

"Shut up now!" McConnell said to Falk. "If you open your mouth I'll kill you myself!"

Chapter Thirteen

Pike was almost cold enough to *demand* the makings of a fire when the same brave who had left him there stepped into the teepee.

"About time," Pike said, standing up.

The Indian motioned him out of the teepee, and then indicated that he was to follow him.

"I just hope you're taking me someplace warm."

He followed the Indian to another teepee, larger than the one he'd just left, and entered. Inside it was so warm that he didn't even care who was there waiting for him. There was a fire in the center and beyond the fire sat a man who could have been forty or sixty. His skin was pulled taut over his skull so that the flesh was shiny and seamless, and his cheekbones looked as if they were going to burst through the flesh of his face at any moment. His hair was black, streaked with gray. Pike took a look behind him to see if the other Indian had entered, and found that he had not.

"Sit," the Indian commanded, so Pike sat. He didn't mind because it got him closer to the fire.

"I am Black Cherry Joe."

Pike wasn't sure he heard right, so he frowned and sat forward. Had the man actually said that his name was Black Cherry Joe?

"You do not find that funny?" the Snake Indian

asked.

"If that is your name," Pike said, "it would be impolite for me to laugh at it."

The man's face was impassive, but Pike felt that he had scored a point.

"It is a name that was given to me by whites when I was a young man," Black Cherry Joe said. "It was meant to shame and embarrass me. I keep it to remind me of those times."

Pike didn't know what to say to that, so he just waited for Joe — he chose to think of the man as Joe — to continue.

"Now there are some other whites who have sought to embarrass me and my people."

Simpson, Pike thought. He did it.

"I have done nothing to embarrass you, I assure you," Pike said.

"There were four men," Joe said, "and they stole forty horses and killed two of my people."

"I am sorry."

"They came from the place known as Bonneville's Fort," Joe said. "Is that where you have come from?"

"Yes."

"Did you know what they planned to do?"

Pike decided he had to be real careful here.

"I knew," he said, speaking slowly, "that they wanted to steal some horses from the Nez Perce."

"Why have you come out here?"

"I wanted to stop them."

"You are far from the Nez Perce camp."

"I know," Pike said. He started to speak slowly, trying to explain why he had strayed so far from the Nez Perce camp, but Joe stopped him by holding up his hand.

"You don't have to speak slowly to me," he said. "My English is excellent."

"I can hear that," Pike said. "Excuse me, I meant no offense."

Speaking more normally, he explained about figuring that Simpson and his men might have decided to avoid the Nez Perce and instead steal the horses from the Snake Indians. It wasn't until after he had finished that he realized how that might have sounded. It was as if he was saying that the Snake Indians made easier pickings than the Nez Perce.

"I feel that when one member of a tribe offends, the others must make amends," Black Cherry Joe said.

"And that means?"

"I have sent some braves after the white men who stole our horses," Black Cherry Joe said, "but I still have enough braves to send against Bonneville's Fort."

"Why would you do that?"

"The answer is very simple," Joe said. "I hate whites. What these four white men have done gives me the excuse I need to kill whites."

Once again, Pike wasn't sure he was hearing right.

"How can we avoid this bloodshed?"

"Easily," Joe said, "bring me the four men, and the horses they stole."

"But you have sent braves after them."

"You will have to catch up."

"But by the time I do, the whites might be dead."

"Then you will have failed."

"And you'll attack the settlement?"

"Yes."

Pike looked into the man's eyes and could see the hatred there, a hatred that went back many years and had a lot to do with the name this Indian chief still went by. Could Black Cherry Joe have been sitting on his hatred for that many years, waiting for an opportunity like this?

"You are wondering if I have enough braves to attack the settlement," the Indian said to him.

"No, I'm not," Pike said. "I'm wondering how soon

you will let me go so I can get started. I want to avoid bloodshed among our people."

"Ah, I have you at a disadvantage there," Black Cherry Joe said. "You see, I do not!"

"What do you want?" the Nez Perce brave asked in English. "Why are you here?"

The brave was tall and muscular, probably in his early thirties.

McConnell decided to play it straight and tell the truth. Most Indians respected that.

"We were looking for your camp."

"Why?"

"To warn you."

"About what?"

"Four white men who might be after some of your horses."

The Indians frowned at him. McConnell looked around at the other eight braves, but couldn't tell whether or not they could understand what was being said.

"And you wanted to warn us about this?" the Nez Perce brave asked. "You would have been exposing your own people to danger."

"I know."

"Why would you do that?"

"Because I don't like them," McConnell said, "and because I want to avoid trouble between your people and mine—my real people, that is, the people at Bonneville's Fort."

"We exist in peace with the people of the settlement," the brave said.

"And we would like to keep it that way."

The brave looked puzzled, so McConnell decided to forge on.

"Has anyone tried to steal your horses?"

"No."

"And you have seen no other white men in the area?"

"None."

McConnell looked at Falk and said, "Our journey was unnecessary."

"Huh?" Falk said. "Oh, yeah . . . good thing, huh?"

"Yeah," McConnell said. "Good thing." He looked at the brave and said, "Our business is finished, then. We have warned you."

"And you would like us to let you go?"

McConnell stared at the brave and asked, "Why would you not?"

"I do not know if I believe your story."

"Why else would the two of us come out here, hopelessly outnumbered?"

"I do not know."

"Believe me," McConnell said, "we only came out here to warn you, or to stop those men."

The Indians studied McConnell and Falk and then said, "I cannot prove otherwise." He took a step back and said something to the other braves that McConnell couldn't understand.

"What did he say?" Falk asked, but McConnell ignored him.

"You may go," the brave said.

"What is you name?" McConnell said.

"I am Brave Bear."

"You have made a wise decision, Brave Bear," McConnell said. "I am called McConnell, and I wish you well."

"Go, Mack-connell," Brave Bear said, "before I change my mind."

Pike got back to Bonneville's Fort a day early and was surprised to find McConnell there waiting for him.

"Want a beer?" McConnell asked.

"Desperately."

When they both had a beer in front of them they traded stories.

"I don't know whose experience was worse," Pike said, "yours or mine?"

"Black Cherry Joe?" McConnell said. "Are you — was he — serious?"

"Oh yeah," Pike said, "he was dead serious."

"Don't say that word," McConnell said, closing his eyes.

"How was Falk?"

"Useless, totally useless," McConnell said. "He's a big talker, and that's all."

"Still," Pike said, "he did know where the Nez Perce and Snake Indians were."

"He stumbled on both locations by accident," McConnell said.

"While drunk?"

McConnell nodded.

"Well, we'll have to talk to Kenyon about this, but whichever way it goes we've got to leave in the morning," Pike said.

"Do you think we can catch up to Simpson and the others?"

"They're driving forty head," Pike said.

"To where?"

"Now *that* is a good question," Pike said.

"There are only so many routes they can take with forty head," McConnell said "and they can't be going very far."

"They'll probably have to follow the river," Pike said. "Two men moving fast could probably catch them easily."

"Sometimes I think I can read your mind," McConnell said. "You don't even want to stop and talk to Kenyon. You want to get outfitted again and leave."

Pike slapped his friend on the shoulder and said,

"By golly, you *can* read my mind — almost. No, we'll talk to Kenyon and tell him where we're going. It'll take him some time to get some men together, but while he's doing that we can get a head start."

"They'd never catch up to us before we catch up to them," McConnell said, "so it's the same thing. I'm right, anyway. It will be as if we never told him."

Pike granted him that fact and went on.

"You get us outfitted and I'll talk to Kenyon." Pike stood up and finished his beer in two quick gulps.

"And Sandy," McConnell said, also standing up, "if I'm any good as a mind reader."

Pike grinned back at his friend and said, "And Sandy. I want to check on how Sam and Rocky are doing."

"Oh, I know that," McConnell said, tapping his head with his forefinger. "What other reason could you have for wanting to see her?"

Pike made a rude noise at his friend and they went their separate ways.

Chapter Fourteen

"Pike."

"Hi, Sandy."

Sandy had been leaning over Whiskey Sam's bed and she straightened when she saw Pike enter.

"You're back already?"

"Back," Pike said, "and ready to leave again."

"Why?"

"It's hard to explain," Pike said. "Let's just say we shouldn't even be back here. we're losing ground even as we speak."

She left Sam's bedside and approached Pike.

"Why do I get the feeling that you're an educated man?" she asked.

Pike reacted as if she had poked him in the stomach.

"Where did that come from?"

"Sometimes you talk just like any other mountain man, and other times you say things like, 'even as we speak.' Why is that?"

"I . . . wasn't born in the mountains."

"Where were you born?"

He hesitated, then said, "Do we have to discuss this now?"

"Can we talk about it when you come back?"

"Well . . . sure."

"That's all I wanted to do," she said.

"What?"

"Start a conversation that would be unfinished. Now I know you'll come back to finish it."

Now he had time to think up a good answer.

"How are they?"

She turned to look at the beds, then turned back. "No change."

"Is that right?" he asked. "I mean, for them to go so long without change?"

"No," she said, "it's not. Mr. Victor has shown some signs of coming around. He woke once, but was incoherent. He hasn't awakened again since then."

"And Sam?"

"He just continues to . . . sleep," she said, helplessly.

"All right," Pike said. "I'll be heading out with Skins."

"Going after those men?"

"Yes," Pike said. "They stole some horses from the Snake Indians."

"Not the Nez Perce?" she asked. "I thought I heard talk —"

"They intended to steal from the Nez Perce, yes," Pike said. "That fact has gotten around, huh?"

"I guess so."

"Well . . . I have to go," Pike said. "I have to talk to Kenyon."

"Don't forget," Sandy said, "we have some talking to do, too."

Pike nodded uncomfortably and backed out of the room.

Kenyon listened to what Pike had to say and did not react at all the way Pike expected.

"Black Cherry Joe?" he said, not doing a very good job of stifling his laughter. "I'm supposed to worry that we'll be attacked by a band of Indians led by a

96

man named Black Cherry Joe?"

"Kenyon, listen," Pike said, "never you mind Black Cherry Joe. Simpson and his friends did steal horses from the Indians, and they did beat up Whiskey Sam and Rocky Victor, almost killing them."

Kenyon waved his hands and head at Pike.

"Pike, Pike," he said, "if they stole horses from the Indians, let the Indians try to get them back. As for Sam and Rocky, we still don't know for sure who beat them up. I can't—"

"Jean-Luc," Pike said, "the Snake Indians hold this entire settlement responsible. Black Cherry Joe—don't laugh about this!"

"I can't help it," Kenyon said. "Everytime you say Black . . . Cherry . . . Joe . . ."

Pike sat at Kenyon's table and watched the man laugh uncontrollably. He knew it was hopeless, and he was disappointed in the man.

"Kenyon," he said, standing up, "I'm going to go after Simpson and the others, get the horses back to the Snake Indians, and then I'll take care of them for what they did to Sam and Rocky. I'll probably also be saving this settlement, although I don't know why I bother. With you as leader, and with your attitude it's not going to last much longer, anyway."

Kenyon stopped laughing and stood up abruptly. His face reflected nothing but anger now.

"What do you know about being a leader, Pike?" he demanded. "You never stay in one place long enough to find out. I've got a lot of people depending on me—"

"—and thank God I'm not one of them!" Pike said.

Kenyon started around the table and Pike held up a hand to him.

"Don't start a fight with me, Kenyon."

"I can take you, Pike."

"Maybe," Pike said, "but your little house here wouldn't survive it."

97

"Go on," Kenyon said, "you and McConnell go on your little wild goose chase, but don't bother coming back here when it's over."

"Or what?" Pike said. "You'll throw us out? If you'd had that attitude when Simpson and his bunch arrived, none of us would be in the spot we're in."

Pike turned and left without waiting for a reply from Kenyon.

Pike met McConnell in front of the trading post. McConnell had gotten them two fresh horses and just enough supplies to be split between them and carried by each comfortably.

"Did you see Kenyon?" McConnell asked.

"I did," Pike said, accepting the reins of his horse from McConnell.

"And?"

Pike mounted up and looked down at his friend.

"We're on our own."

"Well, we knew that," McConnell said, "until he gets enough men together . . . right?"

"No," Pike said "The burden of leadership is weighing heavily on Jean-Luc Kenyon."

"He's not going to take action?"

"He thinks the whole thing is funny," Pike said. "He thinks the settlement being attacked by Indians led by a man named Black Cherry Joe is funny."

McConnell mounted up and said, "I wonder how funny he'll think it is when people start to die. I mean, even if he turns the Indians away, somebody is going to get hurt—probably killed."

"Well, I guess we'll have to see that it doesn't happen," Pike said.

"Did big Chief Black Cherry Joe give you a time limit?" McConnell asked. When he got a sharp look from Pike he said, "Sorry."

"No," Pike said, thinking back. "No, I guess he's just going to wait whatever he feels is a logical length of time before he attacks."

"He's going to be logical?" McConnell said.

"The man may be driven by hatred, Skins," Pike said, "but I think he'll give us a chance to succeed." He stared at his friend and said, "He wants us to fail, but he'll give us some time to try and succeed."

"And then when we do fail, he'll take great comfort in it."

"Right," Pike said, "great comfort and a lot of satisfaction."

Chapter Fifteen

Simpson, Brick and Graves looked up as they heard a rider approaching, and relaxed when they saw that it was Al Nudger. He had backtracked to see if they were being followed by anyone.

"Well?" Graves asked as Nudger dismounted.

Nudger paused and said, "You mind if I get a cup of coffee first?"

Graves glowered at Nudger while the big man took his time pouring himself a cup and then sipping it.

"Well?" Graves asked, again.

Nudger ignored Graves and Brick and turned his attention to Simpson.

"I can't see any sign that we're being followed, Derek," he said. "You think those Indians are just gonna give up?"

"Maybe," Simpson said, thoughtfully.

"You got something on your mind?" Nudger asked.

"Maybe . . ." Simpson said, again. "I just wonder if maybe the Indians won't go directly to Bonneville's Fort, maybe hold them responsible for what happened."

"Why would they do that?" Brick asked.

"Because to an Indian," Simpson said, "a white man is a white man."

"That means they might wipe out the whole settlement for what we did," Graves said.

Nudger looked down at Graves with disdain and said, "Does that bother you?"

"No . . . no, not at all," Graves said, shifting uncomfortably. He looked at Brick, as if he were seeking support, but Brick suddenly found the coffee in his cup very interesting.

"All right," Simpson said, "let's get this fire out and move on. I want to reach the river before nightfall."

"We gonna follow the river?" Nudger asked.

"It's the best route."

"Where are we meeting the buyers?"

"Don't worry," Simpson said, "I'll let you all know when we get there."

Simpson had been withholding the name of his buyers right from the beginning, and he wasn't about to give it out now. He didn't want anyone getting the idea that maybe they could make the deal without him.

Simpson didn't trust anyone.

Black Cherry Joe looked up as three braves entered his teepee. For the past forty years he had thought of himself only as Black Cherry Joe. He did not even remember what his name was before that time.

"We are ready," Little Horse said.

"I am not," Black Cherry Joe said.

"But you said we would move against the whites at the settlement."

"I have given my word to the big white," Joe said.

"Your word to a white man?"

"My word is my word," Joe said, "no matter who I give it to."

"What did you promise him?"

"Time to return the horses, and bring us the men who stole them and killed our brothers."

"What else did you tell him?"

"That I sent braves after them."

"But you did not."

"No."

"Then you lied to him."

"Yes."

"Then why should you keep your word?" Little Horse said. "Let us attack the settlement and take our revenge for what their people did."

"The lie did not affect my word," Black Cherry Joe said. "I gave it to the big white, and I will keep it."

That didn't please Little Horse, but Black Cherry Joe was the leader and there was nothing he could do about it — for the moment.

Leadership changed hands, though, and Little Horse was always on the lookout for the opportunity to bring that about.

"Very well," he said, "we will wait."

"I am pleased that you agree," Black Cherry Joe said, sarcastically.

Little Horse withdrew, and the other two braves with him.

Black Cherry Joe knew that his name affected others in different ways. There were those among his people who respected him for keeping the name. He knew they felt that only a brave man would be able to carry such a name. Others, he knew, thought him foolish — like Little Horse. The younger brave was always ready to pounce on an opportunity to usurp Black Cherry Joe's leadership.

There were times when Black Cherry Joe was almost anxious for Little Horse to make his move. Sometimes he thought that he would not fight it when it came.

That time, however, was not now.

He looked at his hand, the dark color of it. A long

time ago the whites christened him "Black Cherry Joe" because of the dark color of his skin.

Then he had sworn that somewhere, sometime, whites would pay for the humiliation.

Whites.

Any whites.

Like the ones at Bonneville's Fort.

Soon.

Because of their late start, Pike and McConnell did not get very far before they had to camp. Over coffee they discussed their plans for the next day.

"If we take a short cut," Pike said, "we can cut down on the distance between us and them."

"To do that we'd have to go over some tough terrain, Pike," McConnell said.

"What are you worried about?" Pike said. "You're half mountain goat, anyway. You always have been."

"I know," McConnell said, "and I know how important time is. Simpson probably has some buyers set up, and is driving the horses to meet them . . ."

"But?"

"What?"

"There was a but at the end of that sentence," Pike said. "What's the problem, Skins?"

McConnell thought a moment, then said, "If it wasn't for what they did to Sam and Rocky, I'd say let's forget it. They haven't done us any harm, and Kenyon doesn't seem too concerned about what's happened."

"I know," Pike said, "but they did seriously injure Sam and Rocky."

"I know."

"Skins," Pike said, "if you want to turn back you can. No hard feelings."

"I know that, Pike," McConnell said, "and you know that I wouldn't do that, because I know you wouldn't turn back with me. I wouldn't leave you to go after them alone."

"I appreciate that."

"I know you do. Hand me that coffee pot, will you?"

Pike passed the pot over and McConnell poured another cup and passed it back.

"Think we're being watched?" McConnell asked.

"I'm sure of it."

"Snake?"

"No doubt."

"I wonder how long Black Cherry Joe will wait."

"I don't know," Pike said.

"I wonder why he never changed his name."

"Who knows?" Pike said. McConnell frowned and Pike added, "Maybe it was worse before it was changed."

Part Four

The Hunt

Chapter Sixteen

"It's cold," McConnell said.

"I don't need you to tell me that," Pike said, "my feet are telling me that."

Their short cut had taken them up high, over Swenson's Peak, where there was ice and snow all the time. At times they had to walk the horses because the purchase was so bad.

"Tomorrow we start down," Pike said, "and it'll get warmer."

"I wonder how far behind them we'll be when we reach the river."

"We'll find that out when we reach the river."

"And what about these braves Black Cherry Joe says he sent after them?"

"What about them?"

"What happens when we run into them?"

"I don't know," Pike said, warming his hands by the fire without looking into the flames. "I'm not altogether convinced that he sent any braves after them."

"Why not?"

"I don't know," Pike said, "just something about the way he said it."

"You think he was lying?"

"Maybe."

"If he was," McConnell said, "how good could

his word be that he would give us ample time to catch up to Simpson and get the horses back."

"I'll still take him at his word," Pike said.

They finished the coffee and then Pike put on a second pot. They'd set watches, and coffee would be a must through the night.

"I've got another question."

"Ask it," Pike said, "we could use the hot air."

"Ha, ha," McConnell said. "What happens if we catch up to Simpson and the others and they've already sold the horses?"

"Good question."

"I mean whoever the buyers are they're buying the horses in good faith."

"From Simpson?" Pike said. "Who do you think would buy horses from Simpson?"

"You have a point," McConnell said, "the buyers are likely to be in Simpson's class."

"Simpson's in a class by himself," Pike said, "but I know what you mean. They're not about to be giving the horses back."

"Unless we give them the money back," McConnell said.

"Well," Pike said, "I guess we should deal with that situation if and when we come to it."

"I guess . . ." McConnell shifted onto his bedroll and said, "First watch is yours, right?"

"I thought I had the first watch yesterday?"

"No," McConnell said, turning over, "I had first watch yesterday."

Pike stared at his friend's back and mumbled, "I could have sworn I had the first watch yesterday."

McConnell waved a hand and went to sleep. Pike leaned over and poured himself a cup of coffee from the fresh pot.

"It's cold," Graves said.

"How would you feel if you were up there?" Simpson said. He pointed up to Swenson's Peak.

"I can't take the cold," Graves grumbled.

"Then what are you doing in the mountains?" Nudger asked.

"I wonder about that myself," Graves said.

"I'll tell you why you're here," Nudger said. "Because if you left—if you left us—you wouldn't know what to do for money, would you?"

"Don't kid yourself, Nudger," Graves said. "If it wasn't for Simpson, you'd be helpless."

"Oh yeah?" Nudger said, standing up. "You wanna stand up and see who's helpless?"

Graves threw off his blanket and for a moment it looked as if he would take Nudger up on his offer, but then he thought better of it and said, "Forget it."

"Graves—"

"Forget it, Nudge," Simpson said. He was staring up at the peak since he mentioned it. "Look up there?"

"Up where?" Nudger asked.

"Up at the peak," Simpson said. "All of you. Look up there."

It wasn't easy to look up there because the sun was high, but they all squinted and tried.

"What are we looking at?" Nudge asked.

"I don't know," Simpson said. "I thought I saw something . . . but now . . . I don't know. Forget it. Let's get moving."

Graves leaned over and picked up his blanket, rolling it up in his arms.

"Graves, go and help Brick get the horses ready to move."

"Yeah, okay."

As Graves walked away Simpson sidled up next to Al Nudger.

"I thought I saw someone coming down from the

peak," Simpson said.

"So?"

"You know what's on the other side of that peak?"

Nudger thought a moment and then said, "Bonneville's Fort."

"Yeah," Simpson said.

"So?"

Simpson looked at Nudger impatiently.

"We had to go around the peak because of the horses," he said. "Somebody else could come over the peak and close the distance between us real quick."

At last it dawned on Nudger what Simpson was getting at.

"You think someone's following us?"

"It's possible," Simpson said. "Let's keep our eyes open, huh?"

"Sure," Nudger said.

Simpson touched his arm and added, "And our mouths closed?"

"Uh . . . sure, Derek."

"And Nudge, lay off Graves, huh?"

"Yeah, okay, Derek."

"Go saddle our horses."

Nudger went to saddle the animals and Simpson looked up at the peak again. It could have been the sun making him see something that wasn't there, but then again . . .

He was going to start keeping his eyes open real wide.

Pike stayed mounted while McConnell stepped down to check the campfire site.

"Not fully cold yet," he said, putting his hand on it. "We can't be that far behind."

He looked up and saw Pike looking up at Swenson's Peak, from which they had just recently come down.

"What is it?"

"I was just wondering," Pike said, still looking at the peak. "From here you might be able to see two men coming down the peak."

McConnell stood up, looked up at the peak, and had to agree.

"Think he spotted us?"

"I think we'd better be real careful from here on in," Pike said. "Let's just assume that he did see, and knows we're coming."

McConnell mounted his horse and looked out at the running river.

"They might cross at some point."

"If they do, so will we," Pike said.

"Something else on your mind?" McConnell asked.

"We've closed a lot of ground on them, Skins," Pike said. "If there were Indians between us and them, one of us would be sure to spot them."

McConnell looked behind them and said, "What if we got between them and the Indians?"

Pike looked behind them as well, then said, "Like I said, we'd better be real careful from here on in."

Chapter Seventeen

Simpson was steaming mad.

They had lost another horse, and that made it three since they had stolen them.

"Look," Graves said, "we're not wranglers. It's all we can do to keep all forty of them from runnin' off."

"The three that we have lost are comin' out of your end, Graves," Simpson said, "yours and Brick's."

"That ain't fair!" Brick complained.

"Maybe you guys will work a little harder at keeping them together," Simpson said.

They turned at the sound of a horse and saw Nudger riding up on them.

"I couldn't catch it," Nudger said. "The animal is probably on his way back to the Snake Indians."

"Shit!" Simpson said. "Watch these animals!" he snapped at Graves and Brick.

He put some space between himself and those two, and Nudger followed.

"Derek, how much farther to the meet?"

"We'll be there tomorrow," Simpson said. "I don't want to lose another horse, Nudger. You better ride drag."

"Huh?"

"Ride behind the horses. If they start to stray maybe you can get them back."

"Oh, okay, Derek. I'll take care of it. How many head we got left?"

"We've got thirty-seven, and I don't want to lose another one. Understand?"

"Sure, Derek," Nudger said, "I understand, but do they?"

Simpson didn't know if Nudger meant the horses, or Graves and Brick.

"Everybody better understand," Simpson said. "The losses are not coming out of my end."

" 'Course not, Derek," Nudger said, "of course not. It's your plan."

"And it was a good one," Simpson said. "All I needed was competent help."

Nudger brought his horse closer to Simpson's and said, "Maybe after this we ought to go our separate ways, Derek, huh?"

Simpson looked at Nudger to see if he was serious.

"I mean," Nudger said, clarifying his point, "we'd do better without those two, huh?"

Simpson's eyes narrowed as he stared at Nudger.

"What's the matter?" Nudger asked.

"Either you're gettin' smarter, Al, or I'm gettin' dumber."

"What?"

"Never mind," Simpson said. "Let's get these animals moving. We've got plenty of daylight before we have to camp."

"Sure, Derek, sure."

Simpson rode up to the front of the pack to lead the way.

He couldn't believe that it had taken Nudger to make him think the way he was thinking now. Graves and Brick were starting to grate on his nerves, so why hadn't he thought of it before?

A two-way split would be a hell of a lot better than a four-way split.

"There's another one," McConnell said.

Pike looked and saw the horse running toward them, and then swerving to go wide around them.

"That's three," Pike said. "If they keep losing them at this rate they'll do our job for us."

"You think those three will find their way back to the Snake camp?"

"I'm sure of it," Pike said.

"Maybe they'll think we sent them back."

"Maybe," Pike said, "and maybe it'll even buy us some time."

They started forward again, on the lookout for more horses.

"They must be having trouble keeping the horses together," McConnell said.

"So would we," Pike said. "None of us are wranglers."

"That brings up a good point."

"Yeah," Pike said, "I know, I've been thinking about that myself. How are we going to get forty head—minus three, now—back to the Snake Indians without losing some of them ourselves?"

"Maybe we could just let them loose and they'd all go back on their own?" McConnell said, hopefully.

"I don't think we could count on that, Skins," Pike said.

"It was just a suggestion."

"Let's camp here," Pike said.

Darkness was about half hour away and McConnell frowned.

"We've still got a half an hour of light."

"I know," Pike said, "but I've got a feeling."

"We're close?"

Pike looked up at the sky and said, "I don't know. It's just a feeling. Why don't you make camp. I want to scout up ahead on foot."

"Don't be long," McConnell said, taking the reins from Pike, "or I'll have to come looking for you."

"Well," Pike said, "give me an hour at least, okay?"

"An hour."

Pike lifted his head and then said, "Go ahead and make coffee. The wind is blowing in our direction."

"Right."

Pike left McConnell to take care of the horses and make camp and moved ahead on foot. He covered a lot of ground with his long strides. When he saw that he was coming to a bend in the river he slowed down and moved more cautiously. He caught the smell of coffee and heard the horses before he came within sight of them. It was kind of hard to keep forty or so horses quiet.

There was some foliage here near the river and, using it for cover, he got into position where he could look around the bend without being seen.

He recognized Nudger first, because the man was so big it couldn't have been anyone else. He saw the horses, tightly bunched, with a man on either side of them, no doubt Brick and Graves.

There was a man leaning over the fire, grabbing the coffee pot, and when he stood up Pike saw that it was Derek Simpson.

Okay, he thought, now that we've found them what do we do with them?

Pike retraced his steps and found McConnell sitting by a campfire with a pot of hot coffee on it.

"The smell of coffee was driving me crazy," Pike said, accepting a cup.

"You mean—you could smell it—"

"No," Pike said, "not our coffee, theirs."

"You found them?"

"They're around a bend in the river about a mile up," Pike said.

"A mile," McConnell said. "That's too close for comfort. What if they send someone back on foot to look around."

"We'll just have to hope that we've got better eyes and ears than they do."

"What are they doing?"

"Having coffee and trying to keep those horses from taking off on their own."

"So," McConnell said, "now that we've got them, what do we do with them?"

Pike stared at his friend, wondering if he really could read minds, or was it that they had travelled together so often that they were starting to think alike?

"Well, we could go and get them now," Pike said, "but it would be two against four, and they must have a watch set up by now."

"If we try that, somebody might get hurt," McConnell said.

"Like one of us."

"Exactly."

They sat for a while, warming their hands on the coffee cups before drinking hot brew to warm their insides.

"What if we stampeded the horses," McConnell said finally, "and took them in the confusion."

"That would probably work," Pike said, "but after we took them, who do you think would have to round up those horses?"

116

McConnell stared at Pike, and then shrugged and said, sheepishly, "So much for that plan."

"Keep thinking, though," Pike said. "Something may pop out by accident."

"Let's hear you come up with somethin' brilliant," McConnell said, challenging his friend.

"Brilliant, no," Pike said, "but maybe something workable."

"Like what?"

"Like waiting."

"Hey," McConnell said, "there's a good one. How long did it take you to come up with that one?"

"You want to snipe at me," Pike said, "or you want to listen?"

"I'm listening."

"Suppose we just follow along with them for a while, waiting for a . . . situation to present itself."

"You mean let nature take its course?"

"Exactly."

"Okay," McConnell said, "I'll go along, but what if the 'situation' that takes place tomorrow is that they meet their buyers? I mean, we're outnumbered now—"

"Whoever the buyers are," Pike said, "all they want to do is buy horses. They're not going to fight for the horses—at least, not before the animals are theirs."

"Hmm . . ." McConnell said, not satisfied with the scenario as it stood.

"Look, if nothing presents itself, then we'll just have to force the issue, but let's not do it tonight. Let's sleep on it."

"You mean one of us will sleep on it," McConnell said, "while the other stands watch."

"Right," Pike said, "and you have first watch tonight."

"Wait a minute—"

"Don't try that on me again," Pike said, pointing his finger.

"Hey," McConnell said, spreading his hands helplessly, "it's always worth a try."

Chapter Eighteen

In the morning McConnell woke before Pike could shake him. Pike was standing waist deep in the river, washing himself.

The water had to be colder than cold!

"I hate it when you do that," he said aloud.

Pike looked up, water running from his beard and mustache.

"Do what?"

"That," McConnell said, "wash in the ice cold water. It gives me the chills."

"I like it," Pike said, coming out of the water. "It makes me feel alive."

Pike was naked and McConnell could see that his balls and cock had shriveled from the cold.

"You don't look so alive to me," he said, not masking the fact that he was looking at his friend's genitals. "If your countless women could only see you now."

Pike looked down at himself, then smiled.

"At least I'm only like this because of the water," Pike said, "while you suffer from the condition all the—"

"Never mind," McConnell said, standing up. "Did you make coffee?"

"Your wake-up cup is in the pot, boss," Pike

said, dressing, "but drink it fast. I don't want them getting a head start on us."

"They can't outrun us now," McConnell said.

"Maybe not," Pike said, "but I want to make sure they don't reach their buyers before we know what the hell is going on."

"Gotcha."

McConnell had his cup of coffee while Pike got the horses ready to go. By the time the animals were saddled, McConnell had washed out the coffee pot and had it ready to stow away.

"Ready to go," he said, mounting up.

"Let's move along easy like," Pike said, "until we know whether they've broken camp or not."

They started forward at a walk and suspended any conversation to alleviate the danger of being heard.

When they reached the bend in the river that Pike had mentioned Pike signalled with his hand and McConnell nodded and stopped. Pike dismounted, handed McConnell his reins and proceeded to walk to the bend and around it. He was prepared to secrete himself in the same spot he'd used last night, but it wasn't necessary. The campsite that Simpson and his men had used was empty.

Pike came back around the bend and waved at McConnell to join him. When McConnell reached him he mounted his horse again.

"This is where they were," he said, unnecessarily. McConnell could see all the indications that someone had camped there, including the cold fire.

"Let's keep going," Pike said, "but not too fast. I don't want to run up their backs."

"It's too bad we can't get around them," McConnell said.

"Well," Pike said, scanning the terrain around them, "we could, but we'd also be above them."

"To far above them," McConnell said. "We'd be able to see them, even fire at them, but we wouldn't be able to take them."

"We're going to have to do that from here, on level ground."

McConnell looked out at the river and said, "There's another alternative."

Pike saw where McConnell was looking and said, "Cross the river?"

McConnell nodded.

"Let's think about this for a minute," Pike said. "From the way it looks now, we could cross right here, but the river might widen and deepen as we go along. If that happens we'd be stuck on the other side."

"But we could get ahead of them and find another narrow section, and cross back over."

Pike nodded, weighing the pros and cons. He looked at McConnell, and McConnell looked at him, and they both nodded.

"Let's split up," Pike said.

McConnell smiled and said, "Now who's reading minds?"

Simpson felt as if his senses were heightened. He was trying to keep an eye ahead of him, because soon they would be coming to a clearing where he was supposed to meet his buyers. He was also trying to keep an eye out to his right and above, and behind him. Even though he had three men behind him, he wasn't about to count on them to spot someone trailing them.

Simpson wondered who, if anyone, was behind them. Was it the Snake Indians, trying to get their horses back? Or was it someone else, like Pike? If Pike had decided that it was Simpson who was responsible for the beatings his two friends took, then Simpson had no doubt that Pike would follow him. He wouldn't have minded if Pike caught up to them either—but after they did their deal with their buyers. Once he had money in his pocket, getting rid of Pike would be a pleasure, and one that he'd want to give his full attention to.

Pike was just the kind of man Simpson disliked. He was respected by other people, and he looked down on people like Simpson. Pike had everyone fooled—everyone but Derek Simpson.

If Pike was on his trail he probably had Skins McConnell with him, but if Simpson knew Jean-Luc Kenyon, the settlement leader wouldn't commit himself of anyone else unless there was proof—and Pike had none. The two old men who Nudger had beaten were probably dead, and Nudge had said there were no witnesses.

Pike and McConnell, against Simpson, Nudger, Brick, and Graves. First they'd take care of Pike and McConnell, and then Simpson would have Nudger take care of Brick and Graves. All of this, of course, after they met with the buyers.

Simpson had made arrangements in advance of going to Bonneville's Fort. He'd planned all along to steal horses, he just didn't know who they'd be stealing from. He made that decision after he talked to Harry Falk, who was probably a drunken blowhard, but who did know the locations of both the Nez Perce and the Snake Indians.

His buyer's name was Les Roberts, who had made his share of shady deals in his time. Still, Simpson sensed that Roberts didn't like him, and the feeling was mutual. Roberts, a handsome, silver-haired man, thought he was better than Simpson, but he was a businessman and he needed horses to outfit a buffalo hunt. When Simpson heard about his need, he sought him out and made the deal to deliver horses. Roberts had not asked where Simpson would get the horses, but the man probably realized that the animals would be stolen.

That made Roberts no better than Simpson, as far as Derek Simpson was concerned.

Simpson heard some commotion behind him and turned to see what was going on. He saw Graves and Brick fighting to hold the horses in check.

"Nudge, get in there and help them!" he shouted, riding back toward them.

Simpson didn't know the first thing about controlling a herd of horses, but he expected Graves, Brick and Nudger to do it while he stayed a safe distance away.

That was the way Derek Simpson's mind worked.

McConnell watched Pike ride across the river, with no anxious moments, and then waved when his friend reached the other side. After that, McConnell continued riding along the river bank, the only place where the ground was soft enough to hold tracks.

Splitting up had been a mutual decision, but now that it was done and the river was widening, McConnell was wondering if they'd made the right decision. He had not argued much when Pike volunteered to cross the river, which at the time had seemed like the chancy move. Now it seemed that McConnell had taken the bigger chance.

He was in a position where he could be stuck on this side of the river all alone.

He decided not to think about that, and concentrated on following the tracks.

* * *

Pike had ridden his horse into the river tentatively, unsure of what the footing was like, or the depth. As he walked his horse into the water he felt the current tugging at his pants legs. It was strong, but not stronger than the animal he was sitting on.

He reached the center of the river and the water was over his knees. His horse was holding his head high, but did not appear to be in any danger or distress.

When the felt the water fall below his knees, he knew that they had made it. Moments later, he was standing on the opposite bank waving at McConnell.

Pike had volunteered to cross the river, and when McConnell had demanded why it should be he who takes the chance Pike had simply said, "Remember, the water is very cold."

Now he waved at McConnell that he was fine, and they both continued on. For a while they were within sight of each other, but then the river began to widen, and the conformation of the bank began to change. Soon all of that and some foliage caused them to lose sight of each other, and Pike decided to quicken his pace.

He rode on at that pace, casting a frequent glance across the river, which had widened even more. He was starting to think they had made a mistake by splitting up. What if the river never narrowed enough for him to get to the other side again? That would leave McConnell alone on that side of the river to deal with not only Simpson and his three men, but Simpson's buyers, and possibly some Snake Indians.

He quickened his pace even more, hoping that the river would narrow soon.

Even though the decision had been made together, if something happened to Skins McConnell while Pike was on this side of the river, he'd never forgive himself.

Chapter Nineteen

"Here," Simpson said.

They'd turned another bend in the river and suddenly they were in the clearing that faced a sheer rock wall. Even though Simpson was not a horseman, he could see why Roberts had chosen this for their meeting place. The rock wall formed a semi-circle, and once they herded the horses into that semi-circle, they'd be much easier to contain.

"Nobody's here," Graves said.

"We're here," Simpson said. "Push the horses into there," he added, pointing to the rock wall.

"In there?" Graves said.

"Yeah," Simpson said, "in there. What's the matter, don't speak English?"

"Take it easy," Graves said, "we'll put the horses in there."

"And I want both of you watching them."

"Why both of them," Graves said. "Once they're in there we'll only need one man to keep them there."

"I don't want anything to go wrong when we're this close," Simpson said. "Both of you stay on your horses, and watch them."

"Come on, Ed," Brick said, "let's get it done."

Reluctantly Ed Graves backed away from Simpson and followed Phil Brick.

Al Nudger rode up on Simpson and said, "Are we here?"

Simpson glared at him and said, "Don't you start in, too."

McConnell almost rode right up behind the small herd of horses before he realized they had stopped. He backed his horse up and found an outcropping of rocks to conceal himself behind. He dismounted and watched as two of the men — Graves and Brick — forced the horses up against a rock wall, the sides of which came out to form a semi-circle. It was an almost perfect half corral.

This was the meeting place, and Pike was still on the other side of the river.

Great plan.

The river had narrowed, not enough to cross, but enough for Pike to see across. He could see Simpson and the others, and the horses. He looked behind them, but could not spot McConnell.

He followed along for a while, keeping pace, and then suddenly they stopped. They seemed to be herding the horses against a wall, and Pike figured that they had reached their meeting place.

If he allowed himself he could have become frantic. Here he was on this side, and McConnell was on the other side where all the action was going to take place. It was probably deeper than where he'd crossed the first time, but he could cross the river here. Of course, he would be in plain sight of Simpson and his men. They might let him get to their side before making a move, or maybe they'd start shooting at him while he was in the middle of the river, helpless.

He knew that he had to ride on and find someplace where he could risk it, someplace where he could cross so that he'd be there with Skins McConnell when the first shot was fired.

"Hold on, Skins," he said, and kicked his horse in the ribs to get him going.

McConnell scanned the opposite bank, but could not see Pike. If he knew Pike, though, he was there and he knew what was going on. He hoped that Pike wouldn't try to cross the river here, but would find a place farther up to do it. Once he did that, they'd have Simpson and the others in a crossfire.

Come on, Pike, he thought, if we can really read each other's minds, read this . . .

Les Roberts knew the Green River terrain as well as anyone. He'd been there and back so many times that he knew all the landmarks. He knew that he and his seven men were only about a half an hour from the place where they were to meet Derek Simpson and consummate their deal for horses.

Roberts was no fool. He knew that whatever horses Simpson had he would have stolen, probably from Indians. He just hoped that Simpson had not led anyone else to their meeting place.

He stopped and called back, "Bradley!"

Mike Bradley rode up and reined his horse in next to his boss.

"Yeah, boss."

"Ride on ahead and make sure Simpson didn't bring some company with him."

"Sure, boss. Uh, who are we expecting?"

Roberts looked at Bradley and said, "Whoever he stole the horses from."

"Gotcha," Bradley said.

"We'll wait here," Roberts said. "Coffee'll be waiting when you get back."

Bradley smiled. Roberts was probably the best boss he'd ever had, and he would have walked over hot coals for him.

"Thanks, boss."

As Bradley rode off he heard Roberts called out, "Paretsky, make coffee!"

Pike rode a mile before he found a spot he thought he—and the horse—could handle.

It was wider than the point where he'd crossed, and deeper, but he didn't think he could afford the time it would take to keep looking for a better spot. For one thing, if he went any further it would take him a while to get back to Simpson's meeting place.

"Okay, horse," he said, "we're going for a swim."

Mike Bradley saw the man crossing the river and stopped to watch. The man was almost to the middle, and already the water was up to his thighs. Bradley was willing to bet that when he got to the center the water would be up to his waist. That meant that the horse was going to have to lift his head way up, or swim.

Bradley leaned one arm over the other and watched with interest. If the man didn't drown, he might get swept away by the current.

Bradley made a mental bet with himself, and settled down to watch.

Right away Pike knew that the current was stronger than before. The horse leaped in the water as a branch being carried by the current struck him on the rump, but Pike retained control of the animal.

They were almost to the middle when Pike saw the man on the opposite bank. He couldn't afford to give the man his attention, but he didn't seem to be doing anything but watching.

As they reached the center Pike gave the horse his head. The animal would know whether it had to swim or not—Pike just hoped it knew how!

Pike sat up straight on the horse and held his Sharps in one hand, high above his head so it wouldn't get wet. He also held his powder horn in the same hand, but he knew that if the current became more of a problem, and if the bottom suddenly fell away, he'd have to drop both and worry about himself.

"Keep your powder dry," was often used as a way to wish someone luck, or to say goodbye.

Sure.

So was drowning.

For a moment Bradley thought the man had lost it, especially with his hand held over his head keeping his powder dry, but then he caught his balance and started moving with the horse.

The man knew how to ride a horse.

Pike almost lost it for a moment. He was ready to release his gun and powder, and then caught his balance. Suddenly, the swimming horse seemed to

130

find purchase, and they were walking again.

The water began to recede, down to his waist, his knees, and then his calves. Suddenly, they were on the opposite shore, and Pike was very much out of breath.

Why should I be out of breath, he wondered as he slid from his horse's back and lay on the ground, when the horse did all the swimming?

Chapter Twenty

Pike was lying on his back, trying to catch his breath, when a man appeared above him, looking down.

"Nice job," the man said.

"It could have been easier," Pike said.

"How?"

"Next time I'll get a bigger horse."

The man laughed and extended his hand. Pike took it and the man helped him to his feet. The man, who appeared to be about six feet tall, looked up at Pike's full height and said, "My friend, you need a bigger horse."

"Right now," Pike said, "I need to dry off."

"Take off your clothes and lay them out," the man said. "The sun'll dry 'em."

"I don't have time for that," Pike said.

"Gotta be someplace?"

"Yeah."

"Me, too."

Pike looked at the man and caught himself before he could say anymore. After all, this man could be Simpson's buyer.

"Where do you have to be?" the man asked.

"Uh—"

"By the way," the man said, sticking out his

132

hand, "my name's Mike Bradley."

"Pike."

"Pike," Bradley said, "could you use a drink?"

"I think I've had enough water, thanks."

The man smiled a smile that probably tumbled women over onto their backs with their legs wide open.

"I wasn't talking about water."

He walked to his horse and came back with a half a bottle of whiskey. There was no label on the bottle, but that didn't bother Pike at the moment.

"Here," Bradley said, "take all you need."

Pike took the bottle, slid the cork out and took two good swallows, and then handed it back.

"That's it?"

"That's all," Pike rasped, as the rotgut set fire to his insides.

"So," Bradley said, "you didn't tell me who you were meeting."

"No," Pike said, "I didn't."

He was soaking wet from the chest down, but there was nothing he could do about that now.

He was starting to think that this man might not be the buyer—he didn't look like he could buy forty or so head—but there was a good chance that he was an advance man for the buyer.

"Well," Bradley said, "it's none of my business. I have to get going. Can I do anything else for you?"

"No," Pike said, "no, I think I'll take a moment to catch my breath and then move on."

"Suit yourself," Bradley said. He held up the bottle and said, "I could leave this for you?"

"No," Pike said, "thanks."

"All right," Bradley said.

He walked to his horse, put away the bottle

and mounted up.

"So long," he said, giving a little wave.

Pike watched the man ride away, wondering about him. He seemed a fine, decent man who was out to help someone he thought might be in trouble.

Could this man be on his way to buy stolen horses from a man like Derek Simpson?

Or was he putting on a very good act?

Pike watched the man until he disappeared from sight, then went to check his horse to see if the animal was all right.

McConnell watched as Nudger set up camp, Graves and Brick remained mounted near the horses, and Simpson sat down and did nothing. It appeared that in the division of labor, his job was simply to tell the others what to do. That was why Simpson had chosen those three men to ride with, because they would let him tell them what to do.

McConnell took stock of his situation. He had his rifle and his pistol, which could take care of two of the men, but what of the other two? If he were to jump out now and get the drop on them, would they charge him, knowing that he could not kill all of them.

He decided that he was going to have to wait, either until their buyer came along, or until Pike did. Maybe, if the buyer came first, he could reason with them, explain that lives at Bonneville's Fort depended on his bringing those horses back.

Would that hold much weight against the buyer's need for the horses?

He might have to find that out the hard way.

Pike decided he couldn't take much longer to rest. If he waited much longer things might get away from him.

As he saw it, he had two choices. He could follow Bradley and see if he met with Simpson, or he could go the opposite way, and see if Bradley was indeed the advance man for a larger force.

There was a chance that whoever the buyer was, Pike might know him. Maybe it would be someone that he could reason with. Maybe it would be someone he could talk to, whether he knew him or not.

He mounted up and decided to ride back the way Bradley came. If he came across a main group of men, there would be no reason for them to attack him. They would simply be travelers crossing paths. That move had seemed to work with Bradley, and it would work with anyone he might meet.

As he rode back the way Mike Bradley had come he realized that Bradley might have been just that, just a traveler whose path he had crossed. The man had certainly done him a good turn by supplying that whiskey. He could still feel its warmth inside of him.

If Bradley was the advance man, then Pike was losing nothing by going back the way the man had come, because Bradley would soon be coming back to report his findings to his boss.

Les Roberts was enjoying a leisurely cup of coffee when one of his men, Danny Marlowe, came over to him.

"What is it, Danny?"

"Rider coming, sir." Marlowe, barely twenty, was the only one of Roberts' men who called him "sir."

"It's not Bradley?"

"No, sir."

"Well then," Roberts said, "it seems like we have a guest."

"Yes, sir."

"Offer him a cup of coffee, Dan," Roberts said, "and the comforts of our camp."

"Yes, sir."

"And have Catlett join me."

"Yes, sir."

Marlowe went to intercept the rider, and Catlett came over to the fire.

"You wanted me?"

Catlett was probably the ugliest man Roberts had ever seen. He wasn't tall, not much beyond five-eight, but he was wide and powerful, and if every force of men had to have a enforcer then that's what Catlett was, Les Roberts' enforcer.

"We have a visitor coming into camp.

"One of Simpson's men riding advance?"

"I don't know," Roberts said, "but keep an eye on him, okay?"

"Sure."

"Just keep an eye on him, Catlett," Roberts said. "Don't do anything unless I say so."

"Sure, Les, sure," Catlett said. "That's what you pay me for, isn't it?"

Chapter Twenty-one

Pike stopped when he saw a man—or a boy—approaching him. Obviously, his approach had not gone unnoticed.

"Hello," the boy called.

"Hello."

As the boy came closer Pike saw that he might have been as old as twenty, which technically qualified him as a man.

"We have a camp up ahead," the boy said. "My boss has asked me to invite you for a cup of coffee, since you'll be passing right through us."

"That's very friendly of him," Pike said. "I accept your offer."

"Good," the boy said, smiling. He turned his horse and said, "Follow me."

He followed the boy's lead into a camp where there were about six men. Counting the boy, that would make seven, and if Bradley was one of them, eight.

He dismounted and handed his reins to one of the men, then followed the boy to the fire. There was a white-haired man holding a cup of coffee, and another man, an ugly man who was as wide as a bull.

The man with the white hair did not appear to be old, perhaps forty or so, so the white hair was probably not a sign of age.

The other man struck a chord with Pike. He did not know him, but from the way he looked, Pike thought he might be a man called Catlett.

He hoped he was wrong.

"Hello," the white-haired man said. "Welcome to our camp."

"I appreciate your offer of coffee," Pike said.

"You look like you could use it," the man said. "Did you fall in the river?"

"Crossed it."

"Here," the man said, "have a cup."

Pike accepted the cup and took a healthy swallow.

"My name is Les Roberts," the white haired man said.

While the man's appearance had not registered with Pike, his name did. He hired out to people who wanted to go on hunting trips. From what Pike remembered, he supplied everything from rifles to horses, for a price.

This, then, must be Simpson's buyer.

Mike Bradley watched the four men carefully, and picked out Simpson fairly easily. He was the only man who was sitting down doing nothing. Bradley didn't think he could ever ride with a man like Derek Simpson, not after riding with Les Roberts. He didn't even know how Roberts could do business with the man.

From his vantage point Bradley could not get an accurate count of the horses, but there seemed to be thirty-five or forty of them, which was what the deal had been for. Apparently, Simpson had come through.

Bradley backed away and mounted his horse. He had the information his boss needed, and now he needed a cup of coffee.

McConnell was getting fidgety. If Pike was looking for a place to cross the river, he probably had to go a long way. If the buyers showed up, McConnell knew he was going to have to make some kind of move.

The problem with that was, his mind was coming up blank.

"Pike," Pike said, introducing himself.

"Well, sit down, Mr. Pike," Roberts said. "Take some warmth from the fire."

Pike sat and finished the coffee.

"Let me fill that for you again," Roberts said.

"Thanks."

Pike was aware that the man he thought was Catlett was watching him carefully. Now Roberts seemed to be studying him.

"I don't think I have a man in camp your height," Roberts said, "but I might be able to offer you a dry shirt."

"That's okay," Pike said. "This one is drying."

"Suit yourself."

Pike took another swallow of coffee and headed off what he thought was going to be a question.

"I might have run into one of your men downriver a bit."

"Oh?"

139

"Fella named Bradley, Mike Bradley?"

"Yeah, Mike is one of mine. Good man."

"He was there with a bottle of whiskey when I needed it."

"Pulled you out of the water, did he?" Roberts asked, laughing.

"Just about."

"That's Mike," Roberts said, "always ready to share his last drop of whiskey with a stranger who needs it."

"Are all your men like that?"

"Oh, God, no," Roberts said, laughing. He looked up at Catlett, and then back at Pike. "Take Catlett, here. He wouldn't share a thing with you if he didn't have to. In fact, he'd just as soon kill you as look at you."

"Catlett," Pike said.

"You know me?" Catlett asked.

"I've heard of you."

"Yeah?" Catlett said. "I've heard of you, too, Pike."

"Have you?"

"You know Pike?" Roberts asked.

"Mr. Pike here," Catlett said, "he's a legend, like his friend, Jim Bridger."

"Is that a fact?" Roberts said, looking at Pike differently. "Are you a really true legend, Mr. Pike?"

"I hardly think so."

"Modesty," Roberts said. "Only a true legend of the mountains could be so modest."

Pike drank coffee.

"You know, I might have a place for you, Mr. Pike," Roberts said. "I could use you in my business."

"I know what your business is, Mr. Roberts,"

Pike said. "You see, I've heard of you, as well."

"Really?" Roberts said, looking surprised . . . and pleased. "I'm flattered."

"What possible use could I be to you in your business?" Pike asked.

"You're being modest again, sir," Pike said. "Do you know how many people, how many tenderfeet, would want to hunt with you, with Jack Pike? Do you know how many people would pay for that privilege?"

Pike took a moment to drain the coffee cup. He had to find some way to get Roberts to let him ride with him to Simpson's camp. Maybe he could talk the man into turning the horses over to him and McConnell.

"Tell me," Pike asked, "would some of that money be finding its way into my pocket?"

Roberts laughed.

"Even legends have money trouble, huh, Pike?"

Pike smiled.

"Even legends have to eat, Mr. Roberts."

"I suppose so," Roberts said. He looked up at Catlett and said, "What do you think, Catlett. Should I hire Mr. Pike, here?"

"Sure, why not?" Catlett said after a moment. "After all, you won't be hiring him to do what I do."

"And just what is it that you do, Catlett?" Pike asked the wide man.

Catlett smiled, turning an ugly face even uglier, and said, "You better hope you never have to find out, Pike."

Pike looked at Roberts, who simply smiled and shrugged.

"Do you want to work for me, Mr. Pike?"

"I might consider it, Mr. Roberts."

"Why don't you ride along with us for a while, then, Mr. Pike, while you make up your mind?" Roberts said. "That is, unless you were going somewhere in particular when you rode in here?"

"I guess I'll do that, Mr. Roberts," Pike said.

Mike Bradley rode into camp and was surprised to see Pike sitting there drinking coffee.

"I hope you left some of that for me, Pike," he said.

Pike looked at Roberts, who said, "There's plenty. Hunker down here and have a cup."

Roberts poured his man a cup and handed it to him.

"I hear you and Mr. Pike ran into each other downriver a way."

"We did," Bradley said. "He was dragging his horse across the river."

He and Roberts laughed and Pike just smiled.

Catlett didn't laugh or smile. He was still watching Pike very carefully.

"What'd you find, Mike?" Roberts asked.

Bradley opened his mouth to speak, then thought better of it and looked at Pike.

"It's all right, Mike," Roberts said. "Pike is gonna be riding with us for a while."

"Glad to hear it," Bradley said, raising his cup to Pike. He looked at Roberts then and said, "The horses are there, just where they're supposed to be."

"Simpson?" Roberts asked, and Pike did his best not to react to the name, since Catlett had eyes only for him.

"He was there," Bradley said, "with three other men."

"Anyone else?"

"Not that I could see, boss."

"Okay," Roberts said, "good work. Finish your coffee and we'll get moving."

"What's this about horses?" Pike asked.

"We're buying some," Roberts said.

"From a man named Simpson?"

Roberts was in the act of rising and slowed down, looking at Pike.

"You know Simpson?"

"I've heard of him," Pike said.

"What have you heard?"

"That he's a troublemaker," Pike said, carefully, "and a thief."

"I know that about him," Roberts said, "tell me something I don't know."

"And you're still willing to do business with him?" Pike asked.

"I need horses, Pike," Roberts said, "and Simpson said he could supply them. From what Bradley just told me, he's kept his part of the bargain. I intend to keep my part, as well."

Pike shrugged and said, "Hey, who you do business with is your business."

"That's right," Roberts said. "It is. As long as you remember that, we'll get along."

As Roberts walked away Pike thought that he doubted that very much.

Pike stood up and Catlett moved into his path.

"You and me," Catlett said, looking up at Pike, "I don't think we'll ever get along."

"Why not?"

"I don't like you, Pike," Catlett said.

"Well, Catlett," Pike said, "you aren't the first man to dislike me, and you sure won't be the last."

"Maybe not, Pike," Catlett said, "but I'm the worst. You'll see."

As Catlett walked away from him Pike shook his head.

"What did I do to deserve that?" he asked Mike Bradley, who had finished his coffee and stood up.

"You're taller than he is," Bradley said. "Catlett hates anyone taller than he is."

"You're taller than he is."

"And he hates me," Bradley said. "In fact, a lot of people are taller than he is, but he seems to have made some sort of snap judgment about you."

"I guess so."

"If I was you, I'd keep a watch on my back."

As Bradley walked away Pike thought, as if I didn't have enough trouble, already.

Chapter Twenty-two

"So where is this guy?" Nudger asked.

Simpson looked up at Nudger from the water. "He should be here shortly," he said.

Nudger hunkered down by the fire and asked, "What are we gonna do first, Derek — I mean, after we get the money for the horses?"

Simpson looked over to where Graves and Brick were sitting astride their horses, looking impatient and more than a little annoyed.

"Well," he said, "the first thing you're gonna do is kill Graves and Brick."

Nudger stared at Simpson and asked, "Uh, why am I gonna do that?"

"Because," Simpson said, slowly and patiently, "a two-way split is a lot better than a four-way split . . . don't you think?"

Nudger thought it over, then grinned and said, "Well, sure."

"Good," Simpson said. "You don't have any problem with killing them?"

"Hell, no," Nudger said. "Is there any particular way you would like me to do it?"

"No," Simpson said, "I'll leave that to you.

145

Think about it."

"Okay," Nudger said.

The big man stood up and walked away, presumably to think it over. That was good. If he was thinking of how he could kill Graves and Brick, it would never occur to him that Simpson might be thinking of killing him, too.

Simpson had not made that decision, yet. If he killed Nudger that would leave him alone, with no one to talk to, no one to give orders to. He wasn't yet sure he wanted to do that. After all, even if he did split the money with Nudger, he'd have easy access to it. It would be the same as if it were all his.

He turned and looked behind him, in the opposite direction from where they had come. He looked up at the sky and figured that Roberts was about a hour late.

He'd be here, though. He needed those horses. He'd be here.

Simpson wanted to get this thing over with.

McConnell watched as Simpson and Nudger had a conversation, and then Nudger walked away. Simpson looked behind him, then, and McConnell figured the man must be getting impatient.

An idea dawned on McConnell then. What if he were to get the drop not on all four men, but on Simpson. If he had Simpson as a shield, would the others disarm themselves when told to? They might, but the trick would be to get to Simpson without the other three knowing it, and that was highly unlikely. He'd have to walk through the camp to get to Simpson, and he didn't think he could do that without the other three seeing him. Graves and Brick were busy with the horses, but Nudger was just wandering around at this point. The big man would be sure to see him.

He'd have to come up with another plan.

Not likely. It had taken hours to come up with that one.

Where was Pike?

Pike mounted up and waited for the others. He considered riding with the pack, trying to fit in and put everyone off guard, but disregarded the idea. He wasn't going to be with them long enough for that to matter. He decided he'd ride up front with Roberts, maybe keep up a running conversation with the man. While he was doing that he was going to have to come up with a plan and hope that McConnell would be able to go along.

As they started off, Pike rode up on Roberts' right and the man looked at him curiously. He was probably used to riding alone, with the others behind him. Pike held his breath and waited to see how the man would react.

To his relief, the man started a conversation.

"So, what were you doing most recently, besides traveling?"

"Some hunting," Pike said. "I wintered on the Yellowstone."

"Did you?" Roberts said. "Was the hunting good?"

"It was excellent, but it was probably the coldest winter I ever spent."

"The cold bother you?"

"Not normally," Pike said. He didn't elaborate. He didn't think Roberts would be interested in hearing about the ordeal he and McConnell went through on the Yellowstone.

As they rode on they discussed different regions where they had each done some hunting. The whole time Pike was aware of Catlett riding behind him. It was like riding with some malevolent presence just behind his right shoulder. It was all he could do to keep from turning around and looking at the other man every five minutes.

Luckily, the situation wouldn't last much longer. He hoped.

They rode on at a leisurely pace for about twenty minutes and then Bradley rode up and joined Roberts and Pike on the front end.

"It's just a little farther, boss."

"All right, Mike," Roberts said. He stopped, and everyone behind them stopped, as well.

"How do you want to play this?" Bradley asked.

Roberts thought for a moment, then said, "I'll ride in first, with Catlett and . . . Pike." He looked at Pike before continuing. "I don't want to spook them."

"Why should they be spooked?" Pike asked.

"Knowing Simpson," Roberts said, "there's a very good chance that he stole these horses from someone. That means that someone is probably looking for them, or him and his men, or all of them."

"Aren't you worried about being caught with stolen horses?"

"I didn't steal any horses," Roberts said, "and I'll have a bill of sale to prove it. In the absence of any real law, I think that'll stand up. If it doesn't, we can always make it stand up."

Pike didn't respond, and Roberts chose to interpret that as agreement.

"Mike, you bring the other men in when I give you the signal."

"A single shot?"

"That'll do," Roberts said. "Of course, if you hear more than one shot, come a-runnin'."

"We will, boss, don't worry."

"And don't jump the gun, son," Roberts added. "We may have some dickerin' to do, and it might take a while."

"Okay, boss."

"Good man," Roberts said, slapping Bradley on the shoulder.

"Isn't the price already set?" Pike asked.

"It is," Roberts said, "but that don't mean there won't be some last second hagglin'."

"Roberts."

The speaker was Catlett, and both Roberts and Pike turned to look at him.

"What is it, Catlett?"

"I think you and I should ride in alone."

Roberts nodded and regarded Catlett silently for a moment.

"Your suggestion is noted," he said, finally, "but I make the decisions around here. Pike will ride in with the two of us. Understood?"

"Sure," Catlett said.

"All right," Roberts said. "How's your pistol

after your swim?" he asked Pike.

"Wet," Pike said, "but my rifle and powder are dry enough."

"Good," Roberts said, "you'll ride on my left, Catlett on my right."

"Let me get something straight before we start," Pike said.

"All right."

"Are we going to buy the horses from Simpson, or take them from him?"

"That's a fair question," Roberts said. "I'm here to buy horses, Pike, but if Simpson should cause any trouble, I'm not averse to taking them from him. I'm a man of my word. Does that answer your question?"

"Perfectly. There's one other thing."

"What's that?"

"Simpson and I don't get along."

"Well," Roberts said, "that should serve to make things more interesting, don't you think?"

Pike smiled grimly and said, "At the very least."

"All right," Roberts said, "let's go."

Pike took a deep breath and gently gave his horse his heels.

Whatever was going to happen was about to happen.

Chapter Twenty-three

Reactions to what happened over the next few minutes were varied.

As Les Roberts, Pike, and Catlett rode into Simpson's camp, Simpson stood up. Nudger came over to stand next to him, but Nudger reacted to no one but Simpson.

Simpson saw Roberts first, and then he saw Catlett. A chill went down his spine, because even with the huge presence of Nudger next to him, Simpson feared the foreboding Catlett.

And then he saw Pike.

"What the hell —" he said.

McConnell, still observing from hiding, saw the three men ride into camp, and recognized Pike immediately. Obviously, his partner had somehow insinuated himself into the company of Simpson's buyers. It was clear that Pike was not a prisoner, that he was there of his own free will.

How Pike had managed it, McConnell didn't care. He knew that Pike would have some kind of plan, and he had to be ready to react.

The total relief he felt he managed to push away, for the moment.

Pike was tense as they rode into camp. He had no idea how Simpson would react to his presence, or how Roberts would react to Simpson's reaction.

"That's Pike!" Simpson said.

"Where?" Nudger said, frowning.

"There, you idiot!" Simpson said, pointing. "Right there."

"Who are the other two?" Nudger asked.

"Never mind."

Graves and Brick saw the three men ride in, and neither one of them really registered Pike's presence. He was hidden momentarily by the other two men. They did see, however, that Simpson seemed to be agitated.

"Is that the buyer?" Graves asked.

"I don't know," Brick said, "but if it is, Simpson don't seem too happy about it."

Graves hefted his rifle and said, "Let's wait and see what happens."

McConnell was mentally measuring the distance between him and Simpson, between himself and Graves and Brick, and between Simpson and the other two men. He decided he was going to have to get closer if he was going to move when Pike did.

152

He knew Pike had a plan.

Pike always had a plan.

Pike didn't have a plan.

At least, when they rode into camp he didn't have a plan, but as they approached Simpson and Nudger he got an idea. It was a crazy one, and it probably had no chance in hell of working, but it was all he could think of.

He put his hand on his Kentucky pistol, and then remembered that it was wet.

Why hadn't he taken the time to dry it?

"What's he doing here?" Simpson demanded.

"Pike?" Roberts said. "He works for me."

"Since when."

"Since about an hour ago," Roberts said. "Do I have to clear my employees with you, Simpson?"

"He's no employee," Simpson said. "He's after me."

"For what?" Roberts asked.

"For . . ." Simpson started, and stopped abruptly.

"Pike told me you and he didn't get along, Simpson," Roberts said. "Why don't we just leave it at that and get on with business?"

Simpson looked at Pike, wondering what was going on. If Pike was after him, how had he gotten ahead of him? Had he come alone? Not likely. McConnell was probably around somewhere. Suddenly, he remembered seeing — or thinking he saw — someone coming down from Swenson's Peak.

153

"Where's the other one?" he asked.

"What other one?" Roberts asked.

"His partner, McConnell."

"Look, Simpson," Roberts said, "I came here to buy some horses—"

"No," Simpson said, looking around, "something's wrong, here."

"Catlett . . ." Roberts said.

"Nudge . . ." Simpson said.

It would have been interesting to see Nudger tangle with Catlett, but Pike was going to have to put a stop to this right now, before things got out of hand.

He lifted his Sharps so that it was pointing at Roberts and said, "Let's all just sit quiet for a minute."

"Pike, what—" Roberts started, but then saw Pike's gun pointing at him.

"Pike, damnit—" Simpson started, reaching for the pistol in his belt.

Pike had to run a bluff. He drew his Kentucky pistol from his belt and pointed it at Simpson.

"Don't, Simpson."

Pike waited for Roberts to call out that the pistol was wet, but he didn't.

"Now what?" was all Roberts said.

McConnell saw Pike draw his pistol and decided to break from hiding. He started running toward the camp, and everyone turned as he broke into sight. Luckily, they were all pretty surprised to see him, and by the time they recovered he had his rifle pointed at Simpson.

"All right," he said, aloud, and the look he

154

gave Pike said, now what?

Pike had heard the question before, and he still didn't have a good answer for it.

Part Five

The Dilemma

Chapter Twenty-four

"Let's not anybody make any foolish moves," Pike called out, loud enough for Graves and Brick to hear him.

"You want to tell me what's going on?" Roberts asked Pike.

"I told you," Simpson said, "he's after me."

"You told me," Roberts said, "but now I want him to tell me."

"Take your hand away from that gun, Catlett," Pike said.

"Catlett," Roberts said. "Don't do anything stupid, huh?"

Catlett moved his hand away from his pistol. His rifle was sitting across his lap, but it was pointing away from Pike.

"I think the first thing we should do is dispose of all non-essential guns," Pike said.

McConnell stared at him and said, "I hate it when you talk fancy like that."

"Everybody drop their guns!" Pike said.

McConnell nodded. That he understood.

"Now, wait—" Roberts said.

"Mr. Roberts," Pike said, "I think we'd all be

better off if there weren't so many guns around, don't you? I'm not looking for anybody to get hurt."

"He wants to kill me!" Simpson shouted.

"Simpson," Pike said in disgust, "if I wanted you dead, you'd be dead."

Roberts looked around, taking stock of the situation, and then shrugged.

"I'll start," he said, and dropped his rifle to the ground. He smiled at Pike and said, "I have no pistol, I'm afraid."

"Catlett," Pike said.

Catlett stared coldly at Pike.

"Drop them, Catlett," Roberts said. "I want to hear what's going on."

For a moment Pike didn't think Catlett was going to do it, but finally the ugly man dropped the rifle, and then the pistol.

Pike looked at Simpson. His rifle was already on the ground at his feet, as was Nudger's.

"Simpson, have your other two friends drop their weapons."

Simpson firmed his jaw stubbornly.

"Derek," Pike said, "if somebody pulls the trigger at the wrong time, you'll be the first to die. If you want to put your life in their hands, that's your business. Personally, the idea would give me the chills."

Simpson turned and shouted, "Graves, Brick, drop your guns."

The two men gave each other confused glances. They weren't close enough to hear what was being said, and they didn't know what to do.

"Drop 'em, damn it!"

They looked at each other again, and then dropped their weapons.

"Either of them carrying pistols?" Pike asked.

"No," Simpson said.

"All right," Pike said. He took a moment to consider the situation. He considered having the mounted men dismount, but being on horseback might put them at a disadvantage. At least, he preferred dealing with Catlett while his feet were off the ground.

McConnell backed away from Simpson and Nudger a bit so that he could swing around and cover Graves and Brick at a moment's notice.

"Do you want to explain this to me, now?" Roberts asked. "Are you robbing me?"

"I'm not robbing you, Mr. Roberts," Pike said. "I'm trying to keep you from making a big mistake."

"My big mistake, I think, was in trying to do business with Simpson."

"Well," Pike said, "now I'm trying to save you from making a bigger one."

Roberts heaved a sigh and asked, "Who did he steal the horses from?"

"The Snake Indians," Pike said.

Roberts looked around, as if expecting to see a bunch of Indians at any moment.

"If they're not here now," Pike said, "they might be here any minute."

"I see," Roberts said. "You're trying to protect me, out of the goodness of your heart?"

"No," Pike said, "I'm trying to protect the people at Bonneville's Fort."

"I've heard of it," Roberts said. "On the other side of Swenson's Peak, isn't it?"

"Right," Pike said. "The Snake Indians are holding the people at the settlement responsible for the actions of these men."

"How can they do that?"

"A white man is a white man, to them," Pike said.

"That sounds like Indian logic," Roberts said. He'd had some dealing with Indians in the past — Nez Perce and Crow, primarily — and there was very little the red man could do that would surprise him.

"Unless we get these horses back to the Snake Indians," Pike said, "they're going to attack the settlement."

"I see," Roberts said. He looked at Simpson with an expression of distaste, and then looked away, pondering the situation.

"Tell me," he said, finally, "how does that affect my need for these horses?"

"It doesn't," Pike said. "There's more."

He told Roberts what Simpson — and probably Nudger — had done to Whiskey Sam and Rocky Victor.

"He can't prove that!" Simpson said.

Roberts looked at Pike and raised his eyebrows.

"He's right," Pike said, "I can't — not unless I take them back with me and one of my friends has recovered enough to identify them."

"So you want to take back the horses and Simpson and his friends."

"Right."

Roberts hesitated a moment before speaking.

"Well, I don't see any problem with taking them back," he said, finally, "but I need these horses, Pike. I'm afraid I can't let you take them."

Pike raised the barrel of his gun and said, "I'm afraid you don't have a choice."

Roberts smiled and pointed to Pike's gun.

"When you fire that, the rest of my men will come riding in. I'm afraid you'll be a little outnumbered when that happens."

"Maybe so," Pike said, "but you won't be around to see what happens after that."

Roberts studied Pike for a few moments, and then said, "You don't bluff, do you?"

Pike hoped that Roberts wouldn't remember that, just moments before, he had been pointing his wet pistol at Simpson.

"Not a hell of a lot," Pike said.

"Well then, we've got us something of a dilemma here," Roberts said.

"A what?" Simpson asked.

"A problem," Pike said, "and yes, we do. I've got even more of a problem then anyone. I've got to get these horses back to the Snake Indians with just myself and Skins McConnell here to drive them. That is, unless . . ."

Roberts laughed shortly and stared at Pike in disbelief.

"I don't believe the gall—you're about to ask me for my men to help you, aren't you?"

"The thought had crossed my mind," Pike said. "In fact, I was going to ask you to come with us."

"Now why would I do any of that?"

"Well, I don't know how soon you need

163

those horses, but surely you could wait four or five more days and then buy them from the Snake Indians after we return them."

Roberts stroked his jaw, then removed his fur cap and ran his hand over his white locks.

"That's an interesting proposition," Roberts said. "And it would get all of us out of here in one piece."

"That it would."

"Don't listen to him," Simpson said. "You've got more men. Let's take 'em."

McConnell moved forward and poked Simpson in the back with the barrel of his rifle.

"You'll be the first one to go, Simpson."

Simpson blanched, and Nudger—calm as could be—watched his boss for some sign of what to do.

Catlett was also calm, but Pike didn't think he was waiting to be told what to do. The ugly man was probably just waiting for a chance to do what he wanted to do.

"That sounds like the best way out for all of us, Mr. Roberts," Pike said. "I know that if I kill you, your men will probably ride in here and kill me. Simpson will end up dead, too. That'll leave your men and his men not knowing what to do, and they'll probably kill each other out of sheer ignorance."

"You paint a bleak picture, Pike," Roberts said.

"You have the power to change it," Pike said.

"What if I agreed?" Roberts said. "Would we get our guns back?"

"You would."

"What makes you think we wouldn't take you somewhere along the way?"

"You'd give me your word you wouldn't."

"And you'd take me at my word?"

"Yes, sir," Pike said, "I would."

Roberts shook his head at Pike and said, "By God, you have gall."

"Maybe I'm just stupid."

"No," Roberts said, "I don't see that as an option."

"What's it going to be?" Pike asked.

Roberts took a moment to think it through clearly, and then nodded.

"All right, we have a deal."

"Let's make it real clear."

"My men and I will go back to Bonneville's Fort with you, and help you deliver the horses to the Indians, and these men to the settlement."

"After that you'll try to buy the horses from the Indians?"

"I'll give it a try," Roberts said. "It isn't my favorite option, but you do have the drop on me."

"How does that sit with you?"

"The fact that you got the drop on me?" Roberts asked. "I'm impressed, sir. There are only two of you, and between Simpson and myself a dozen men, and you and your friend are in control. I find that very impressive."

"I'm afraid Catlett is not as impressed as you are," Pike said. "He strikes me as being a man with a mind of his own. Will he go along with this?"

Roberts looked at Catlett, whose face was

expressionless.

"Catlett works for me," Roberts said.

Somehow, Pike didn't find that as comforting a reply as he would have liked.

Chapter Twenty-five

It was an uneasy alliance, to say the least.

The ones who liked it the least were Simpson and his men. Their hands were tied behind them and they were released only to eat. Their legs were not tied.

"Where would they run to?" Roberts had asked, and Pike agreed.

Roberts put a man on guard over the four of them while they ate, while he ate with Pike, McConnell and Mike Bradley. The food from Roberts' supplies was the best Pike and McConnell had had in days, and he had enough to share with them.

"I always travel well prepared," he'd said.

"I should have known you were trouble the minute I saw you," Bradley said to Pike, good-naturedly.

"I'm glad you didn't," Pike said. "You might have thrown me back in to drown."

"I might have, at that," Bradley said, laughing. "Tell me about the Snake Indians?" Roberts said. "How many would be on our tail?"

"Well," Pike said, a bit sheepishly, "to tell you

167

the truth we haven't really seen any Indians along the way."

"Why you lying bastard . . ." Roberts said, but his smile took the sting out of it.

"For all we know the whole bunch of them are out looking for their horses . . ." McConnell said.

"But we sort of doubt it, huh?" Roberts said.

"They'd need most of their men if they were to attack the settlement," Pike said.

"Who's their leader?" Roberts asked. "Maybe I've heard of him."

That was the question Pike had been dreading, but he answered it honestly.

"Black Cherry Joe is his name."

Bradley broke out into laughter immediately, but Roberts only smiled.

"What's in a name, anyway?" he said. "Who's in charge at the settlement?"

"Jean-Luc Kenyon."

"Ah," Roberts said, "him I know. Jean-Luc used to be pretty wild."

"That was before he became booshway of the settlement," Pike said. "He's calmed down quite a bit. In fact, he's become downright conservative."

"Wouldn't send anyone with you, huh?"

"He was unconcerned about the Indians because of the name of their leader," Pike said. "Can you believe that?"

"And he wouldn't send anyone after Simpson and his men because he had no proof that they had beaten up anyone, right?"

"Exactly."

"Come on, Pike," Roberts said, "you can't exactly blame him for that, can you?"

"That's what I told him," McConnell said.

"I guess not," Pike said, "but he's going to feel pretty scared and silly if the Indians attack the settlement."

"Well," Roberts said, "maybe we'll get back there in time, eh?"

Pike looked across the fire at Roberts and said, "You're taking this real well."

"You outmaneuvered me, Pike," Roberts said. "I can admire you for that, but don't think that means I'll forget it. We'll cross paths again somewhere down the road. Count on it."

Pike looked away from Roberts at Catlett, who was off to himself, eating alone.

"Has he worked for you long?" he asked.

"Ah, Catlett," Roberts said. "He's the only man I've ever met who has no redeeming virtues. A man like that comes in handy, at times."

"I find that hard to accept," Pike said.

"Oh, believe me," Roberts said, "there have been many things I've wanted done that I couldn't do myself. With Catlett, all I have to do is point him in the right direction—like a gun—and pull the trigger."

"What happens when you can no longer control him?" Pike asked.

"I pay him," Roberts said. "The man with the money is always the boss, Pike, don't you know that by now?"

"I'm afraid I don't accept that either Roberts."

"Les," Roberts said, "call me Les, Pike—and I see that we have some fundamental differences in our beliefs. That doesn't mean we can't be friends, does it?"

Pike studied Roberts for a moment, wondering how the man could be so good natured after the

169

way he'd forced him into going along. Roberts did not strike him as the kind of man who enjoyed being forced into something. Pike had no doubt that, somewhere down the road, he'd have to pay a price for this.

He just hoped the price wouldn't be too steep for him to handle.

They turned in, and Roberts wanted to set the watches with his men. Pike insisted that he and McConnell be included in the watches.

"As you like," Roberts said, "but I hope you don't expect me to take a watch. There are some advantages to being the boss, you know."

"Take all the advantages you have coming, Les," Pike said.

"I intend to."

There were four two hour watches. Mike Bradley took the first, McConnell the second, a man named Haywood the third and Pike the last. During that last two hours Pike kept a wary eye on the four prisoners, the man who was watching them—a watch which was also divided into four shifts—and he especially kept an eye on Catlett.

The entire two hours he was certain that Catlett was awake, lying in his bedroll, staring at him. He didn't know why Catlett had taken such an instant dislike to him, but it had probably intensified when he got the drop on him and Roberts. Catlett was not likely to be so forgiving as Les Roberts was.

Pike had the feeling that before this was all over he and Catlett were going to go at it.

It was not something he was looking forward

to.

At first light Pike woke McConnell, and together they woke the others. Pike was particularly interested to see how Les Roberts would react to the new day. Would he have second thoughts about the deal they'd made after having slept on it?

If Roberts wanted to go back on his word he could have done it the day before, right after Pike returned his and Catlett's gun, and after the rest of his men had ridden into camp. He hadn't done it then, and Pike didn't think he'd do it now.

At least, he hoped he wouldn't.

It was necessary to put on two pots of coffee so that everyone could have some, but they decided to skip breakfast and get moving. Roberts suggested that Bradley ride on ahead, just in case they were riding smack into a band of angry Snake Indians. At least that way they'd get some warning. Pike had no argument with that.

It was left to the rest of Roberts men to drive the horses, and Pike could see how much easier it was for them, because they knew what they were doing.

Because they had to work the horses, Pike and McConnell rode with Simpson and the others between them. Roberts rode at the front of the pack, as he always did, and Catlett off to one side, alone. Pike decided that if Catlett was going to make a move on him, it would be when this was all over, so he figured he'd ignore the man for the time being so that his attention wouldn't be diverted from the task at hand.

When they camped for the night Pike voiced an idea that had come to him during the day's ride.

"I think someone should ride over Swenson's Peak and get back to the settlement ahead of the rest of us."

"Who do you think that should be?" Roberts asked.

"I think it should be Pike," McConnell said. "He's the only one Black Cherry Joe knows."

Roberts looked at Pike.

"You think you can convince him not to attack the settlement on your word that the horses will arrive in two or three more days?"

"I hope I can," Pike. "Maybe I can get him to ride part of the way and meet the rest of you."

"McConnell told me that this Indian hates whites, that he's looking for an excuse to kill some."

"That's true," Pike said, "but I don't think he's crazy."

"Which means?"

"He'll wait until he's got a damned good excuse, and he won't go making one up."

"You've got a lot of faith in an Indian who would keep a name like Black Cherry Joe."

"I've got a lot of faith in a lot of people."

"That's right," Roberts said. "You'd be leaving McConnell here with the rest of us."

"Seems to me that's more my problem than his," McConnell said.

"That's right, Skins," Roberts said, "it is.

You're willing to go along with this?"

"I guess I'm like Pike," McConnell said. "I've got faith in certain people."

Roberts regarded them both for a moment and said, "Well, by golly, I'm flattered."

"Bull," Pike said.

Roberts laughed and spooned himself some more bacon and beans, poured himself another cup of coffee.

"All right," he said, "why don't you start over the peak in the morning, Pike. The rest of us will keep driving the horses to the settlement."

"Not to the settlement," Pike said. "I'll meet you at a certain point and show you where to lead the horses."

"Fair enough."

"One more thing."

"What's that?"

"I don't want to go alone."

"I'll send Bradley with you—"

"No," Pike said, "I know who I want."

"Who?"

"Simpson."

Roberts digested that for a moment and then said, "I can see why. With Simpson, Black Cherry Joe might see his way clear to waiting."

"That's the way I'm thinking."

"Well, it sounds good to me, Pike," Roberts said. "I wonder how Simpson will like it."

"Not that he's got much choice in the matter," Pike said.

Pike kept the news from Simpson until they were ready to break camp the next morning.

"Let's move out," Roberts called.

Simpson's hands were tied in front so he could handle his horse. As he started to move forward Pike grabbed the horse's reins and said, "Not us."

"Whataya mean, not us?" Simpson asked.

"We're going that way," Pike said, pointing up at Swenson's Peak.

Simpson looked up at the Peak, and then back at Pike.

"Oh no, I ain't goin' there with you," he said, firmly.

"Why not?"

"You're gonna kill me up there," he said. "Probably throw my body off the peak."

"Can't you get it into your head, Simpson?" Pike said. "If I wanted you dead you'd be dead."

"What the hell are we goin' that way, for?" he demanded.

"To stop a massacre."

Simpson's eyes widened and he said, "You're gonna give me to the Indians."

Pike smiled and said, "Black Cherry Joe is waiting for you, Simpson."

"Jesus—" Simpson stammered, "—Pike, you can't—I'm a white man, for Chrissake—you can't hand me over to a redskin!"

"Sure I can," Pike said. "Watch me."

"That'd be murder!"

"No, Simpson," Pike said, "that'd be justice."

Chapter Twenty-six

Pike had taken a minimum of supplies. Also he didn't plan on camping but once, so that they'd make it up and over the peak in about twenty-four hours.

"This is crazy," Simpson said. "We gotta stop and rest."

"We will," Pike said, "soon."

"My horse is gonna die."

"Your horse is fine."

"I'm gonna die!"

"Oh, don't worry, Simpson," Pike said, "I'm not going to let that happen—not yet, anyway."

When they reached the top Pike called a halt to their progress and camped.

"It's freezing up here," Simpson complained.

"Enjoy the cold," Pike said. "As long as you can feel it, you're alive."

"Pike," Simpson said, his teeth chattering, "we gotta talk about this."

"Here," Pike said, throwing him an extra blanket, "it's more than you deserve."

Simpson took the second blanket and wrapped it around him with the first, then moved closer to the fire.

"This ain't what I was talkin' about," Simpson said.

"I know what you were talking about," Pike said.

"You can't turn me over to Joe Cherry."

"Black Cherry Joe."

"Whatever his name is!" Simpson said, frantically. "You can't give me to him."

"Did you have to kill some of his braves when you took the horses?"

"Two Indians," Simpson said. "Two! Is that enough to die over?"

"A life is a life in my book, Simpson."

"They was Indians, damn you!"

Pike ignored him and poured out a cup of coffee. He hated to do it, but he passed it to Simpson. He didn't want the man freezing to death before they got back.

Simpson grabbed the coffee, spilling some on his hand, but he didn't seem to mind the heat.

"Look, Pike," he said, after drinking half the coffee, "I'll make you a deal."

"What kind of deal would I want to make with scum like you, Simpson?"

"Take me back to the settlement," Simpson said. "Turn me over to Kenyon."

"And what do I get?"

"I'll tell him who beat up your friends."

Pike stared at Simpson.

"Sure," Pike said, "you'll give up Nudger and expect to walk away."

"Nudger beat them up!"

"But you told him to."

"I never—"

"Shut up, Simpson," Pike said. "Finish your coffee and get some sleep. I want to get an early start in the morning."

Pike should have expected it, but he didn't. Simpson was so frantic that he should have seen it coming.

"No," Simpson screamed, "you can't!" And with that he threw the remainder of his hot coffee into Pike's face.

It was so cold that Pike barely felt the heat. He felt the wetness strike his face, and was aware that something was burning him, but before he could react Simpson launched himself across the fire, his tied hands reaching for Pike's throat.

Pike took Simpson's full weight and they both went over backward, rolling in the snow. Simpson's hands were on Pike's throat, and for all Pike knew his eyes had been burned out. He reached for Simpson and found that his hands were pinned between them.

Their blankets unravelled and were left behind as they continued to roll in the ice and snow. Simpson was trying to choke the life out of Pike, and Pike was fighting to free his hands. Finally, he pulled one hand free and shoved the heel of his hand underneath Simpson's chin. Using all his strength he pushed back, bending the other man's head back. If Simpson didn't yield to the pressure his neck would break, so he finally released his hold on Pike's throat and pushed away from Pike.

Simpson tried to regain his feet and run but Pike was on him. Much larger and stronger, Pike soon had Simpson down on the snow and was holding his face down in it. Simpson was trying

177

to speak, but the snow was drowning him out. If Pike held him there just a little longer, he'd suffocate and die. Finally, Pike realized this and climbed off the man's back. Simpson rolled over onto his back and began gasping at the frigid air.

"If you do that again . . ." Pike gasped, "I'll gut you and leave you to die. Do you hear me?"

Simpson waved one hand to indicate that he understood. He was even more tired than Pike was, and could not find the strength to speak.

They both remained that way until they caught their breath, then retrieved their blankets and crawled back to the warmth of the fire.

Pike woke Simpson the next morning. His face felt funny and was probably blistered from the hot coffee. His throat ached from the hold Simpson'd had on it last night. Simpson looked at him and seemed to take some small satisfaction from the way he looked.

"Maybe I look bad," Pike croaked, "and sound funny, but you're the one who's on his way to meet his maker. Think about it while we're going down the peak, Simpson. Think about what the Snake Indians will do to you. Believe me, it'll take you a hell of a long time to die at their hands."

"Fuck you," Simpson said.

"Good," Pike said, "you're back to your old self again. I was getting pretty tired of all the whining and begging you were doing."

"I ain't gonna beg, you bastard."

"Good," Pike said, "save your begging for the Snake Indians. They love to hear white men beg."

"Bastard!" Simpson spat.

"Get up and get on your horse," Pike said.

Simpson staggered to his feet and found that his legs were numb from the cold.

"I can't feel my legs."

"Don't worry about it," Pike said. "You don't need them."

He boosted Simpson onto his horse, then tied him to the animal, spreading his hands one on one side and one on the other, so that he sat the horse awkwardly. It would probably cause him some back pain after a while, but soon after Pike handed him over to the Snake Indians, that would be the least of his worries.

Pike mounted his horse, took up the reins of Simpson's and started down Swenson's Peak.

Idly, he wondered who the hell Swenson was?

Chapter Twenty-seven

Black Cherry Joe stared into the fire in the center of his teepee. He was seeing something only he could see. As always, he could see his past reflected in the fire. As hard as he looked, he could never see his future, only his past, replayed over and over again. "Black Cherry Joe" the whites had named him, trying to humiliate him, but Black Cherry Joe refused to be humbled or humiliated. He took the name, kept it, built his hate upon it, and now—many, many years later—he was going to pay back the whites.

Any whites.

Little Horse entered his leader's teepee and waited for the man to acknowledge him.

"What is it?" Black Cherry Joe asked.

"Our braves grow impatient," Little Horse said. "They wish revenge for the death of their brothers."

"And they will have it."

"They have waited long enough—" argued Little Horse before he realized what Black Cherry Joe had said. "They will have it?"

"Yes."

"When?"

"Today."

"When?" Little Horse asked, pushing harder.

"Today, Little Horse," Black Cherry Joe said. "Have them ready. When next I come out, we will go and have our revenge."

"I will tell them," Little Horse said. "They will be pleased."

Little Horse was not pleased, however, Black Cherry Joe knew. He wanted to argue now, and try to take control. That Black Cherry Joe was now ready to move on the whites on the settlement came as an unpleasant surprise to Little Horse.

He would have to wait for another day to become leader.

Three quarters of the way down the peak Simpson's horse suddenly stumbled and fell. Simpson rolled free as the horse tumbled over and over, and came to a stop lying on his side. Pike rode down to them, alert for a trick from Simpson.

There was no trick coming, however. The horse had stepped in some kind of a hole and snapped its leg. Simpson had rolled free of any serious injury, although he was bruised.

Using his Kentucky pistol, Pike put the animal out of its misery.

"Now what?" Simpson asked.

Pike glared at Simpson, taking the time to reload his pistol.

"I'd like to make you walk the rest of the way," Pike said.

"Yeah," sneered Simpson, "but you won't. You

want to get to the settlement and save all those people from the nasty Indians, don't you?"

"You're right," Pike said, "I do."

"That's the difference between you and me, Pike," Simpson said.

"Thank God for that," Pike said.

He approached Simpson and took out his knife. Simpson backed away a few steps, involuntarily, but all Pike did was cut his hands free.

"Wha—"

"Put your hands behind your back."

"Why?" Simpson demanded.

"I'm not going to share a horse with you unless your hands are tied behind you."

"I can't ride with my hands—"

"Don't worry," Pike said, "I won't let you fall, Simpson. Put your hands behind your back."

"I won't," Simpson said, like an obstinate child.

"Either put your hands behind you, or walk the rest of the way."

"You wouldn't make me walk," Simpson said, "it would take too long."

"I'll drag your ass, Simpson," Pike said, harshly, "then the Snake Indians can have what's left when we get there."

Simpson stared into Pike's eyes, which were hard and cold as ice.

"What's it going to be?" Pike demanded.

Simpson hesitated a moment longer, then abruptly turned around and put his hands behind his back.

McConnell was wary.

He did not trust Les Roberts as much as Pike

apparently did, but he had to admit that the man seemed intent on keeping his word.

Catlett was another story. Pike had warned McConnell before leaving to watch Catlett, but McConnell hadn't needed the warning. He knew Catlett's reputation, but he also agreed that Catlett wasn't likely to try anything until this matter was resolved, and when he did it would be of his own accord. Roberts would not be behind it.

"You're worried about Catlett," Roberts said as they camped.

McConnell thought that over and then said, "Wary is a better word."

"No," Roberts said, "you're wary of me, you're worried about Catlett."

"You're right," McConnell said.

"I think you're right to worry," Roberts said, "but not for yourself. He's got it in for Pike, but I don't think he'll do anything until we reach the settlement."

"That's what we figured," McConnell said.

"What will you do," Roberts asked, "you and Pike, if we reach the settlement and it's . . . wiped out?"

McConnell swirled the remainder of his coffee at the bottom of his cup and said, "I don't know. We've got friends there, and it'll be Simpson's fault if it happens."

"Simpson?" Roberts said. "Not the Indians?"

"Why blame the Indians?" McConnell said. "They'd be retaliating against an injustice done to them by whites."

"You'd condone their actions," Robert asked, "wiping out an entire settlement?"

"No," McConnell said, "not condone, but I'd understand it."

Roberts shook his head and said, "You're better men than I am."

"A lot of people would rather blame a red man than a white man," McConnell said.

Roberts opened his mouth to reply, then closed it, thought a moment, and nodded.

"I suppose you're right," he said, finally.

McConnell wondered if Les Roberts had just learned something about himself.

The urgent knocking at Jean-Luc Kenyon's door came at a most inopportune time.

Kenyon was in bed with his wife and was, in fact, nestled comfortably between her legs. Her legs were wrapped around his waist as he drove into her, his hands beneath her, cupping her firm, broad behind. Jean-Luc had always liked his women on the meaty side, and when he married he'd married just that kind of woman. She was built for bed, soft and comfortable to be on top of, big breasts, wide hips and cushiony ass taking his weight very easily.

"What is it?" Kenyon asked irritably, without withdrawing from the vise-like grip his wife had on his swollen penis.

"Mr. Kenyon!" The voice belonged to Tim Champlin, and he was highly agitated. "Mr. Kenyon, please, I have to talk to you."

"Damn," Kenyon said, looking down at his wife. "Damn damn . . ."

She moaned as he withdrew from her, grabbed a pair of pants and went to answer the door.

"What is it, Champlin?" he asked, holding his pants closed with one hand.

"I think you better come quick, Mr. Kenyon," Champlin said.

"What the hell is it, Tim?" Kenyon asked "What's wrong?"

"Indians," Champlin said.

"Where?"

"Right outside the settlement."

"Nez Perce?"

"Snake, I think."

"Snake Indians," Kenyon said. "All right, I'll be right there."

Kenyon rushed back into his house to dress and grabbed up his rifle. His annoyance at the interruption was gone, as was his erection. He was thinking about Pike, and about a man who had once been a man of action, but who might have grown fat and complacent as the booshway of Bonnveville's Fort. Now the inhabitants of Bonneville's Fort might be the ones who had to pay for it.

"What is it, my husband?" his wife asked sitting up in bed.

He looked at her and said simply, "I might have been wrong. Pike might have been right, and I might have been wrong." He stared for the door, then turned and said "God help us, and forgive me, if I was."

Chapter Twenty-eight

Kenyon looked out at the Indians sitting on their horses outside of Bonneville's Fort.

"Anybody get a count?" he asked.

"Gordy Shirreffs counted thirty or so," Champlin said. "I figure they got more than that, they're just showin' us thirty."

"Yeah," Kenyon said, "and maybe that's what they want us to think?"

"Maybe."

"How many men with rifles we got?"

"Maybe seventeen."

"That's all?" Kenyon asked.

"Pike and McConnell are gone, Whiskey Sam and Rocky Victor aren't in any shape. Walt Exman took about six men out hunting with him yesterday morning, they won't be back for a week or more."

Kenyon stared out at the Indians, biting his lower lip in concentration.

"We're going to need whatever women we have that can shoot," he said, finally. "We'll start with my wife."

"But your wife's—" Champlin started to say,

then stopped.

Kenyon knew what he was going to say, that his wife was an Indian. That didn't mean anything. She wasn't Snake, and she'd fight for her home, no matter who it was against.

"Have we got extra guns?" Kenyon asked.

"Some," Champlin said.

"Well, let's find out how many," Kenyon said, withdrawing from the wall.

"What if they attack now?"

"They won't," Kenyon said. "They want us to think about it first. They'll sit out there for hours, if they see fit. Whatever they decide, we've got some time. Let's put it to good use."

Pike and Simpson were down off the peak and nearing the region where the Snake Indians were camped. That is, unless they had moved their camp in response to Simpson's attack on them. If Black Cherry Joe were going to launch an attack on the settlement, he'd want to move his women, children, and elderly someplace safe, first.

"Pike."

Pike ignored Simpson.

"Pike, come on," Simpson said, "we can make a deal."

"Don't start that again."

"I'll confess," Simpson said. "Pike, I'll confess that I told Nudger to beat up your friends."

"Both of them?"

"Whiskey Sam was the one I wanted," Simpson said.

"Why? Because he said something you didn't

like?"

"That," Simpson admitted, "and I wanted to give you something to think about besides me."

"You played that wrong, Simpson," Pike said. "All you did was make sure that all I thought about was you."

"I realize that, now."

"Yeah, well, now is too late for you, Simpson."

"Whataya mean? We can't make a deal?"

"No deal."

"I said I'd confess, damn you!" Simpson said. "What more do you want?"

"I want to hand you over to Black Cherry Joe, Simpson," Pike said, "and let him deal with you."

"Why you—" Simpson said. He began to move about, trying to either throw himself off the horse, or knock Pike off.

Pike leaned back and gave Simpson a shove, tumbling him off the horse to the ground. He hit hard, the air rushing from his lungs.

While he tried to catch his breath Pike looked down at him and said, "I meant what I said on the peak, Simpson. You give me any more trouble and I'll gut you and leave you to die slow. You got that?"

"Uh, yeah . . . yeah . . . uh . . ." Simpson said, still trying to catch his breath. "Pike . . . uh, Pike . . . bastard . . ."

"You'll be calling me worse than that when Black Cherry Joe and his people start working on you."

Simpson, breathing a bit easier now, glared up at Pike and said, "Kill me, Pike. Kill me fast, why don't you? You know you want to."

"No," Pike said, "I won't kill you. That'd be the easy way out for you, Simpson."

"I didn't kill any white men!" Simpson shouted. "I only killed some damned Indians."

"Well," Pike said, "we don't know that for sure, do we? Sam or Rocky could be dead by now, which makes you guilty of murder."

"Take me to the settlement and let's find out, then."

Pike shook his head and dismounted. He lifted Simpson off the ground and forced him back up into the saddle. He was about to mount behind him when Simpson suddenly kicked the animal in the ribs, and the horse sprang forward. The sudden movement caused Pike to lose his balance and fall over backward, onto his ass. From there he watched the horse run off with Simpson as a helpless passenger.

With his hands tied behind him Simpson could do nothing to direct the horse, or control him. The animal was running free, and increasing his speed.

Pike got up quickly and began to give chase, but he knew that if the horse kept running he'd never catch up. Cursing himself, he increased his own speed, praying for the animal to stop.

If he lost Simpson the settlement would have to pay for it, and pay dearly.

Simpson felt elation.

He'd done it. He'd escaped from Pike, and now he was free—except that he had no control over the horse.

189

As suddenly as he had felt elated, he felt worried. If he couldn't control the animal he was in danger of being thrown. He clamped his knees together, trying to cling to the animal's back, but as the horse's speed increased, his perch became more and more precarious.

Suddenly, the ground fell away beneath them and they were going down hill. Simpson tried to lean back in the saddle, but it was no use. The horse was rushing headlong down the hill, and they were approaching a collection of rocks and trees.

He succeeded in ducking several overhanging branches, but finally one caught him beneath the chin. His head was jerked back violently and he fell—was catapulted—backward off the horse. When he landed he did so among a collection of different size stones and rocks.

When Pike finally caught up to him he thought that Simpson had broken his neck when he landed on those rocks. The truth of the matter was, Simpson's neck had cracked when the tree limb had caught him under the chin, and he'd died immediately.

The man hadn't felt a thing.

Pike looked down at Simpson's body and cursed the man loudly, with feeling. He leaned over and grabbed the man by the shirt front.

"You're not going to get away with this, Simpson," he shouted into the dead man's face, as if Simpson could still hear him. "Even dead, you're going to save those people. I swear it!"

Pike looked around and saw the horse farther

down hill. Having lost its rider it had stopped, and he walked down to get it.

It wasn't over yet.

He walked the winded horse back up the hill, then hoisted Simpson's body up off the ground and laid it over the saddle so that the head was hanging over one side and the feet over the other. He tied it into place there and then mounted up behind it.

It wasn't over yet.

Part Six

The Solution

Chapter Twenty-nine

As it turned out there weren't many extra guns in Bonneville's Fort, but what there was were doled out to the women who could shoot.

"Maybe just the sight of the gun barrels pointing at them will deter them," Kenyon hoped.

Kenyon had his own wife on the wall, so there could be no doubt about the severity of the situation. Women who couldn't shoot were brought forward anyway and showed how to reload.

"What do they want?" Calvin Kerr demanded. "We ain't done nothin' to them."

Kerr ran the trading post.

Kenyon knew why the Snake Indians were out there. Derek Simpson and his bunch had stolen their horses. The Snake Indians wanted revenge, and they didn't care which white men they got it from.

"Why don't you go out there and ask them what they want, Kerr?" Kenyon asked. "Maybe you can trade with them. You got anything in stock that might be worth our lives?"

Kerr grumbled and fell silent.

"Why don't we start shooting?" someone asked.

Kenyon looked around and said, "Who said that?"

There was a long silence and then a lad of about nineteen stepped up and said, "I did," in a voice quaking with fear.

"Son," Kenyon said, "the minute we fire, those Indians will know we've got to reload, and they'll be on us in seconds."

"Well," the boy said, not to be deterred, "what if only half of us fired, and then when they charge in the other half could fire while the first half is reloading."

"What's your name, boy?"

"Martin, sir," the boy said, "Martin Cort."

"Well, Martin, that's a fine suggestion, and if it comes to it, we'll do that, but right now we've just got to wait and see what these Indians want to do. Understand? We're not in any position to dictate to them."

"I understand, sir."

"Fine," Kenyon said, "now why don't you get back behind that rifle of yours, eh?"

"Yes, sir."

"Out of the mouths of babes," Kenyon said, and got back behind his own rifle.

When Pike reached the site of the Snake camp he saw that his worst fears had been realized. They'd up and moved it.

"Asshole," he said, pounding the dead Simpson on the back once in frustration.

He had a choice. He could try and track them to their new camp, or he could ride on to the settlement. He decided that since the camp had been moved, Black Cherry Joe had probably taken his braves to the settlement.

He could have made better time if he dumped Simpson's body, but he felt he needed it as a bargaining point with Black Cherry Joe. He wheeled the horse and started him off as fast as he could go carrying double the weight.

"Why do we wait?" Little Horse asked Black Cherry Joe.

"Can you see them?" Black Cherry Joe asked.

"Of course I can see them."

"Can you see the sweat on their brow?" Joe asked. "Can you smell their fear."

"I smell their fear," Little Horse said. "We all smell their fear."

"Then we wait until the smell of their fear increases," Black Cherry Joe said, "until the smell of fear becomes so sour that it becomes the smell of death. That is when we will attack."

"Thinking about your friend Pike?" Roberts asked.

"Yes."

They were riding together, McConnell trailing the three prisoners behind him. Catlett still rode off to the right, alone, while Roberts' men controlled the horses. Mike Bradley was still riding on ahead.

"He must have reached the Indian camp by now," Roberts said.

"Unless they moved it."

"If they did," Roberts said, "he'll go on to the settlement. I'm sure he'll find the Snake Indians there—unless they've already been there."

"What happens to our deal if they have?" McConnell asked.

"What do you mean?"

"If the Indians have wiped out the settlement, what happens to our deal?"

"Well," Roberts said, "if they've wiped out a settlement of white people you wouldn't expect me to try and buy horses from them, would you?"

"Well . . . no."

"And if they've already wiped out the settlement, I might as well keep the horses I've got," he went on. "What more could they do?"

"What about them?" McConnell asked, indicating the prisoners.

"Well, as far as I'm concerned," Roberts said, "they and Simpson would be your problem—yours and Pike's."

"And you and your men would just leave with the horses?"

"Sure," Roberts said, "why not?"

"No . . . revenge on your part?"

Roberts smiled.

"My revenge—or retribution—against Pike will come some time in the future," he said. "What kind of a man do you think I am, that I would bother both of you when your friends have been wiped out?"

"You're all heart, Roberts," McConnell said.

"I have a heart, Skins," Roberts said. "I'm not all heart, but believe it or not, I have one. I hope everything turns out the way you want it to."

"Yeah," McConnell said, "so do I."

They were still a day and a half from the settlement, much too late to be of any help if things were on the verge of happening.

And he had himself a premonition that it was.

When Pike reached a point from where he could see the settlement he dismounted and tied the horse off. He moved forward, knowing that he'd be able to see Bonneville's Fort from the rise he was on.

What he saw froze his blood.

In front of the fort were Black Cherry Joe and his braves, just sitting astride their horses. Inside the fort were Kenyon and whatever forces he could rally to the walls — which from Pike's standpoint didn't look like much. Undoubtedly, some of the men would be out hunting, he and McConnell were gone, and whatever condition Sam and Rocky were in, they would be in no condition to be of any help.

He expected the Indians to charge at any moment, but they seemed content to wait, probably sniffing at the air for the smell of fear. Black Cherry Joe wouldn't want it to be over too soon.

Neither did Pike.

He didn't want anything to happen until he

could get down there and try to stop it.

He ran back to his horse, mounted up and started off at a brisk pace. He didn't know what he'd do when he got down there, but something would come to him.

Chapter Thirty

"Who's that?"

Kenyon didn't know who had spoken, but he looked out and saw a man on horseback. He was riding awkwardly, and Kenyon saw that he had something draped over the saddle in front of him.

"Who is that?" someone else asked.

Kenyon squinted his eyes. He thought he knew who it was, but he was trying to force his eyes to give him a clearer picture.

"What's he doin'?"

"Where's he goin'?"

"He's gonna get killed!"

As Kenyon watched, the man rode out into the space between the Indians and Bonneville's Fort, and stopped there.

"What the hell—" someone said.

"That's Pike," Kenyon finally said.

"He's gonna get killed," someone said again, and Kenyon didn't see where he could argue the statement.

"Who is that?" Little Horse said.

Black Cherry Joe did not reply. He simply watched as the white man rode his horse out into the space between his braves and Bonneville's Fort. He held his horse sideways, so that he was not facing one side, and could look at both with a turn of his head.

"That white man is crazy," Little Horse said.

The man seemed to have something draped across his horse.

"Wait a minute," Little Horse said, "isn't that —"

"The big white," Black Cherry Joe said.

"I will kill him myself," Little Horse said, but he made no move.

He would not move until Black Cherry Joe told him to.

Pike rode out into the space between the two forces, still not quite sure what he was going to do or say. His appearance, however, seemed to have gained the attention of everyone involved, and if they were all looking at him, then they could not be killing each other.

Yet.

"Okay, Simpson," he said to the dead body sharing the horse with him, "this is the point where you were supposed to help me out. What do we do now?"

Since the body didn't answer, Pike did the only thing he could think of.

He unceremoniously dumped the body to the ground, making sure it fell on Black Cherry Joe's side of his horse.

"What did he drop?" someone asked.

"I don't know," someone else said.

"Mr. Kenyon," Tim Champlin asked, "what the hell is he doing?"

Kenyon looked at Champlin, then at the rest of the people, all watching him with puzzled looks, and said, "Why don't we all just shut up and watch?"

"What does he think he is doing?" Little Horse asked.

Black Cherry Joe was aware that other of his braves were muttering behind him, wondering the same thing.

"If we wait long enough," he said to them, "he will tell us."

"All we have been doing is waiting," Little Horse complained.

Without looking at the other man Black Cherry Joe said, "And we will wait a little longer."

Pike looked down at Simpson's body, then over at the white people in Bonneville's Fort, then at Black Cherry Joe and his Snake Indians.

It was time to do or say something!

Black Cherry Joe saw Pike's eyes catch his, held them for a moment, and then started his pony forward. Little Horse followed his leader, but the others stayed back.

Black Cherry Joe rode up to Pike and stopped his pony just on the other side of the dead body.

Little Horse rode up next to his leader and stopped.

Pike looked at Black Cherry Joe and pointed to the man on the ground.

"There is the man who stole your horses and killed your brothers."

Black Cherry Joe looked down at the body again, and then back at Pike.

"His name is Simpson," Pike went on. "He and three other whites attacked your men and stole your horses. He was the leader."

"He is dead," Black Cherry Joe said.

"Yes."

"You killed him?"

"No," Pike said. "I was trying to bring him back to you alive. He tried several times to escape. When he finally did, his hands were tied behind him. He fell from his horse and broke his neck."

Little Horse spoke then, harshly . . . and loudly.

"Who is to say this is the man?" he demanded. "This could be any dead white man that you are trying to satisfy us with."

"That is true," Pike said, "but it is not so."

"So says you," Little Horse said. "You would say anything to save your people."

Pike decided to ignore Little Horse and looked directly at Black Cherry Joe.

"I give you my word," he said, "this is the man who stole your horses and killed your brothers."

Black Cherry Joe slid down off his horse and leaned over to inspect the body. He flicked Simpson's head back and forth to satisfy himself that he had died of a broken neck, as Pike claimed. After that he got back up on his pony.

"Where are the other three men?"

"They are being brought here by others," Pike said. "I came over the peak, to try to get here in time to avert a massacre."

"Where are the horses?" Black Cherry Joe asked.

"Also being brought by others," Pike said. "They will be here in one more day."

Black Cherry Joe did not respond to this.

"Surely you can wait one more day!" Pike said, plaintively.

"No," Little Horse said, "we cannot!"

Pike ignored Little Horse and kept his gaze on Black Cherry Joe.

Finally, the leader of the Snake Indians spoke.

"We will wait," he said, "one more day."

"We cannot—!" Little Horse started, but Black Cherry Joe gave him a sharp look and chopped at the air with his hand.

"We will wait!"

Little Horse subsided, but glared at Pike with hatred.

"Thank you," Pike said to Black Cherry Joe. He dismounted and started to pick up the body.

"Leave him!" Black Cherry Joe said.

Pike stood up straight and looked up at the man.

"We will take him," Joe said "He is ours."

Pike backed away and nodded.

"All right," he said, "all right."

He mounted his horse and watched as Black Cherry Joe called two braves forward, who picked up the body and took it away.

Black Cherry Joe looked directly into Pike's eyes.

"One more day," he said. "If they are not here by

then, you will join him—and all these whites—" he said, waving his arm to encompass the settlement, "—will join you!"

Pike sat his horse until Black Cherry Joe had turned and galloped off, his people following him. Then and only then did Pike turn his horse and walk it toward the settlement.

After they had admitted him to the settlement Kenyon ran to Pike and said, "What happened? How did you turn them away?"

Pike looked around for someone to take his horse. That done, he faced Kenyon.

"I gave them part of what they wanted," Pike said. "Simpson."

"That was Simpson you dropped from your horse?" Kenyon asked.

"It was his body."

"And they accepted that?" Kenyon asked.

"No," Pike said. "Black Cherry Joe gave me one more day to produce the other three men, and the stolen horses."

"Jesus—" someone said.

"How the hell . . ." someone else was saying as they moved away with the crowd.

"Talk to these people," Pike said to Kenyon. "Keep them on their toes through the night, in case Black Cherry Joe changes his mind."

"But . . . can you produce what you promised in one day?"

"I hope so," Pike said. "I sincerely hope so."

Pike accepted a dinner invitation at Kenyon's

house, but told the booshway that he had some other stops to make.

"All right," Kenyon said, "but at dinner you've got to tell me everything."

"I intend to," Pike said "because this is only going to work if we all pull together."

"Don't worry, Pike," Jean-Luc Kenyon said, "I'll do my part."

"I know you will, Jean-Luc."

Pike could see that the man regretted his earlier decisions, and he had no desire to say "I told you so,"—not at this time.

Pike left Kenyon to address his people. He wanted to go and check on Whiskey Sam, Rocky Victor . . . and Sandy Jacoby.

Chapter Thirty-one

"You old sonofabitch!" Pike said to Whiskey Sam. "So that hard head saved your life, huh?"

"That's what the pretty lady tells me," Sam said. Still in bed, Whiskey Sam looked more frail than Pike could ever remember. "Nudger did a good job on me, but he didn't get it done."

"Have you told Kenyon yet that it was Nudger?"

"Not yet."

"I'll let him know later, and then you can tell him tomorrow."

In the other bed, Rocky Victor looked only a little better.

"I can get out of bed tomorrow," Rocky said. "Sam's got to stay there for at least another week."

"Busted ribs are a bitch," Sam complained, "but the worst thing is there's no whiskey in this place."

"You mean Sandy is keeping you from the fire water?" Pike asked.

"I certainly am," she said. She was standing behind Pike, but he could feel her hand on his arm. He knew she was glad to see him, and was waiting to tell him—show him—in private.

"Well, I'm glad to see you boys are awake," Pike

said. To Sandy he said, "Are they arguing?"

"Like a married couple."

"Oh, then they're almost back to normal."

"I would be back to normal," Whiskey Sam complained, "if I could get my hands on some whiskey."

"I'll see what I can do, Sam."

"Yeah," Sam said, "you got some influence with the warden, right?"

"I don't know," Pike said, turning and looking at Sandy. "I'll let you know."

"You both better get some rest now," Sandy said to them. "Pike, could I see you in the back?"

"Sure," Pike said. "I'll be back to see you boys later."

Whiskey Sam, hidden from Sandy's view by Pike, mimed taking a drink from a bottle and waggled his eyebrows.

"The back," turned out to be Sandy's shack, and as soon as they entered she threw her arms around Pike's neck and kissed him, a long, wet, slow, lingering kiss that would have melted the ice and snow on Swenson's Peak.

"I thought you were dead," she said, her lips still pressed against his.

"Not with this waiting for me I wouldn't be," he said. He pulled her into his powerful arms and kissed her back the same way.

They managed to get their clothes off between kisses and fell onto her bed together. She climbed atop him right away, positioned herself over him and used her hand to make sure he slid in on the first try. She somehow managed to be wet and tight, and he palmed her breasts, popping the nipples between his fingers, as she rode him up and down. At one point she put a hand on each of his knees, which put her hands slightly behind her. This brought her breasts forward and he ran his hands over them, down over her abdomen and belly, back up her sides and to her breasts again. She rode him that way for a while and then he reached for her and pulled her down to him so that he could use his mouth on her. He kissed her, ran his mouth over her neck, her shoulders, her breasts, biting and sucking the nipples until she shuddered and flattened herself against him, riding out the waves of pleasure, and then when he exploded inside of her she started all over again . . .

As they lay quietly together afterward he told her everything that had happened, and everything that was still to happen — if all went right.

"If it doesn't go right we'll all be dead," she concluded.

"I don't think so," Pike said.

"Why not?"

"I don't think Black Cherry Joe has any more braves than he showed today — unless he's getting them from somewhere else. No, I think we're pretty evenly matched. People will die, on both sides, but I don't think we'll be wiped out."

"But those of you out front, with the guns, will be the ones to die, while those of us who can't shoot, who'll be in the back, will survive. That doesn't sound fair."

"Who said life was fair?" Pike said. "If it was I would have gotten Simpson here alive and he would have told Black Cherry Joe everything."

He squeezed her tight and said, "Don't regret the fact that you might survive while others die. We'll need you alive to care for the wounded."

"Will you show me how to shoot?"

"Sure," he said, "after this is all over."

"What good is that?"

"It means you'll be ready for the next time—if there is a next time."

"I want to—"

"Shh," he said, putting his forefinger to her mouth. She opened her mouth and took the finger inside, wetting it thoroughly before allowing it to pop free.

"Come on," he said, "show me how glad you are to see me again."

She smiled lasciviously, slid down and did the same thing to his cock that she had just done with his finger, only she didn't let it free so easily.

Not until she was done with it.

After they left Sandy's shack, both pleasantly exhausted and sated, she went back to check on her patients, and Pike walked over to Jean-Luc Kenyon's house. When he knocked the door was opened by Black Wing, who simply stepped back and allowed him to enter.

"Pike," Kenyon said, coming forward and taking his hand. "God, I'm sorry I didn't listen to you—"

"Forget that now, Jean-Luc," Pike said. "That's in the past. We have to figure out what we're going to do for the future."

"Tomorrow."

"Yes," Pike said. "I'll need some men to ride out with me to meet Skins and the others."

"That'll leave us ill protected," Kenyon said.

Pike explained to Kenyon that judging by what he saw earlier, the Snake Indians were no better manned than they were.

"There was no way we could tell that from here," Kenyon said.

"Of course not," Pike said. "I'm sure that's what Black Cherry Joe was counting on. I'm also sure that he's sure that every Snake Indian is worth two white men. He thinks he's better manned then we are."

"That puts us at an advantage, then."

"No, it puts us at a disadvantage," Pike said. "If he thinks it, you can bet his men do, too. They'll attack without fear. I don't think we'll be as fearless as they are."

"No," Kenyon said, "I agree."

"All right, then," Pike said. "What we have to do is get those horses here as quickly as possible."

"Here?"

"I don't know where their new camp is, and when they're ready they're going to come here. I want them to see the horses out front, waiting for them."

"And the other three men? Who are they— Nudger, Graves and . . ."

"Brick," Pike said. "I'm afraid we'll have to give them to the Snake Indians, Kenyon."

"I hate to do that," Kenyon said. "What will the others think?"

"Hopefully, most of them will think that the men who got them into this predicament will also supply the solution. I think most of them will go along with it if you seem convinced that you're doing the right thing by turning them over."

"Well, I still hate to do it, but it does seem the only way."

"I don't like it, either," Pike said. "Simpson was one thing, but these men only followed him. Still, they're as guilty as he was of killing those Indians—and Nudger did almost beat Sam and Rocky to death."

"They're awake? I should have checked, but I've been too busy to look in on them."

"And ready to talk to you. I told them they could do that tomorrow."

"God," Kenyon said, shaking his head, "I was wrong again—"

"We're all wrong sometime, Jean-Luc," Pike said. "I was wrong in being so hard on you. You had a lot of other people to think of. I should have realized that."

"Pike—"

"Listen," Pike said, "was I invited here for talk, or for dinner?"

"Dinner," Kenyon said, "definitely dinner. You've never tasted Black Wing's cooking, have you . . ."

Chapter Thirty-two

The following day — at midday — Kenyon rode out with Pike and three other men, including Rocky Victor, who insisted on going along.

"I want to see that big bastard's face when he sees me," he said, and Pike and Kenyon got Sandy to agree to let him go.

"Where will we meet them?" Kenyon asked.

"Skins will take them to where the old Snake camp was," Pike said. "We'll meet them there and bring them all back here."

"I know Les Roberts," Kenyon said. "As far as I know, he's a good man."

"I'm not worried about that," Pike said. "I'm just worried about what he'll do to get back at me."

"Somewhere down the line something will come up," Kenyon said, "but I don't think it will be anything too drastic."

"I hope not," Pike said. "I've had about all the drastic occurrences I can handle for a while — starting with how I got here."

They rode to the site of the old Snake camp and made camp themselves. Rocky Victor put on a pot of coffee while two of the other men took care of picketing the horses.

"Keep them saddled," Pike said. "I'll want to light out of here at a moment's notice."

Pike, Kenyon, and Victor sat around the fire, waiting.

"We should hear them before we see them," Kenyon said, "especially if they've got forty horses with them."

So they waited, and watched, and listened, and as the day wore on, Pike started to get worried.

"I've got to go back," he said, finally. He told one of the other men to go and get his horse.

"What for?" Victor asked.

"When Black Cherry Joe shows up and doesn't see his horses, I'm going to have some tall explaining to do."

"What will you say?" Kenyon asked as Pike mounted up.

"I don't know," Pike said. "You just get those horses to the settlement as fast as you can . . . when they get here."

As Pike rode away Kenyon looked at Rocky Victor and said, "If they get here."

"They'll get here," Victor said. "They've got to."

Pike rode back to the settlement and as he approached it he became aware of riders approaching. He looked and saw Black Cherry Joe, Little Horse and the rest of the Snake braves approaching. He stopped and turned his horse to face them.

Behind him nervous men — and women — trained their rifles on the Indians, but they were under orders not to fire until Tim Champlin — left in charge — told them to.

The rest of the braves stopped a distance away, but Black Cherry Joe and Little Horse continued on until they were five feet from Pike.

"I do not see the horses," Little Horse said, with obvious pleasure.

"They're coming," Pike said, "they had some difficulty—"

"Excuses," Little Horse said to Black Cherry Joe.

"I'm not just making excuses," Pike lied. Well, actually it wasn't a total lie. He wasn't just making excuses, he was making lame excuses, but it was to save lives—both white and red.

"They didn't have enough men to drive forty horses," Pike went on. "It's taken them longer than I expected—"

"How long will you let him lie?" Little Horse demanded of Black Cherry Joe.

Black Cherry Joe stared at Pike for a few moments, and then said, "No longer."

He was about to raise his arm to his braves when Pike blurted out, "This one has a big mouth, like a woman," looking at Little Horse. "He probably fights like a woman, as well."

Before Black Cherry Joe could say anything Little Horse let out a war whoop and charged Pike. Pike moved to meet, him, ducked under a swinging tomahawk and grabbed Little Horse around the waist. They both went flying from their horses and hit the ground with Little Horse on the bottom.

The brave was smaller and lighter than Pike, but he was also faster . . . and more slippery. He quickly squirmed out from beneath the bigger man and tried to mount him. Pike rolled away, and the two men got to their feet, facing each other.

As Little Horse charged, Pike intercepted him, grabbed his arm and knew he could have broken it, but that would have ended the fight too soon. He released the brave and they faced off again.

This time when Little Horse charged he was slicker. He feinted right, and as Pike moved to intercept it, he moved left. Pike saw the tomahawk coming, but was only able to dodge part of it. The flint head struck him on the shoulder, and Little Horse had drawn first blood.

But then again, he was trying to kill Pike, while Pike was trying to prolong the battle until the horses arrived.

It went on that way for what seemed like hours but was probably only minutes, and Pike could see that the Indian was tiring. If he carried the man any longer, Black Cherry Joe would realize what he was trying to do.

As Little Horse charged again, Pike swiveled about to get his hip between them. He slammed his hip into Little Horse's midsection, and then using his right arm took the Indian over his hip. It was a wrestling move, and one the brave was totally unfamiliar with.

As Little Horse hit the ground Pike came down on his arm with his knee, forcing him to cry out and release the tomahawk. Pike grabbed the tomahawk, came down on the brave's chest with both knees, and raised the weapon.

"Wait!" Black Cherry Joe called.

Pike waited, as he had intended to do all along. He didn't want to kill Little Horse.

He looked over his shoulder to see why the Snake leader had called a halt to the fight. Black Cherry Joe was not looking at him, but off into the distance. Pike looked in that direction and saw a small herd of horses being driven his way by a bunch of white men. He recognized McConnell, and got up off Little Horse's chest.

"The horses are here," he said, and extended his hand to the man to help him up. After a moment, the brave accepted the assistance, and Pike brought him to his feet and handed him back his tomahawk. Without hesitation Little Horse ran back to his horse and mounted up, and rode to Black Cherry Joe's side. Pike thought that the brave must be feeling embarrassed, but had hope for the man since he had accepted his hand. Maybe he wouldn't have to be looking over his shoulder for Little Horse, after this was all over.

Pike remained on his feet and watched as McConnell and Roberts drove the horses into the space between himself, Black Cherry Joe, Little Horse and the other braves.

McConnell, Roberts, and Kenyon all approached Pike and the two Snake Indians. Behind them they trailed Simpson's three men, Nudger, Graves and Brick.

"There are your horses," Pike said, still unsure about how to address Black Cherry Joe, "and there are the other three men who killed your brothers."

McConnell and Kenyon rode around behind Pike. Les Roberts rode up to Black Cherry Joe and handed him the reins of the three horses.

"These men belong to you, I believe."

"Yes, they do," Black Cherry Joe said, taking the reins.

"And so do the horses?" Roberts asked. He stretched his arms out to encompass the horses, unnecessarily. Everyone knew which horses he was referring to.

"Yes."

"May we talk about my buying the horses from you?" Roberts asked.

Black Cherry Joe looked behind him at Pike, and then looked at Les Roberts.

"We can talk."

Epilogue

Surprisingly enough, after things were resolved with the Snake Indians, things began to go smoothly.

Les Roberts successfully purchased the horses from Black Cherry Joe, and headed out two days later with all of his men.

Including Catlett.

The night before they left found Pike, McConnell, Roberts and all of Roberts' men in the saloon, having a farewell drink, or two . . . or three.

Off in the corner, however, drinking alone was Catlett, and he had his eyes on Pike the entire time.

"What are you gonna do about him?" McConnell asked. He, Pike, and Roberts were sitting at the same table.

"I think whatever I'm going to do," Pike said, rising, "I'd better get it done right now."

As Pike started across the room the betting started.

McConnell said to Roberts, "I'll give you two-to-one Pike drops him."

"In a brawl, or a wrestling match?" Roberts asked

"In here?" McConnell said. "I think we'd better count on a brawl."

"You've got a bet," Roberts said. "I've never seen Catlett lose a brawl."

The entire room watched silently as Pike walked to the barrel Catlett was using as a table.

"Catlett," he said.

Catlett looked up from his drink and said, "Pike."

"I think if we're going to get it done," Pike said, "we should get it done now."

Catlett thought it over and said, "Sounds good to me."

The only problem both men had was that they were each drunk, to some extent.

"Wait," Pike said, weaving, "let me sit for a minute."

"Bull," Catlett said, "get up on your feet like a man."

He started to rise, but his body would not cooperate and he fell back into his seat.

Across the room McConnell said, "If neither of them can stand, they'll never resolve anything."

"Sure they will," Roberts said.

He stood up and walked across the room to where Pike and Catlett were sitting.

"I have a suggestion," he said.

Pike looked up at him and said, "So, suggest."

"Arm wrestling," he said. "Neither of you will have to get up for that."

Pike looked at Catlett and said, "Are you game?"

"I'll tear your arm off."

Roberts cleared the top of the barrel and

watched as both men planted an elbow. Pike's arms were longer, so he had to move his elbow back some, but Roberts finally had their hands clasped tightly.

"Ready ... set ... go ..."

Catlett rode out with Roberts the next day, satisfied that something, at least, had been resolved.

"Remember," Roberts said to Pike, "you've still got me to contend with."

"I'm trying to forget," Pike said.

When Whiskey Sam was back on his feet Pike and McConnell decided it was time to head out. Kenyon tried to talk them into staying, but knew it was no use. Pike and McConnell had wings on their feet, and would never settle in one place.

McConnell spent that last night at Lottie's, with Flower, the Indian girl.

Pike spent it with Sandy.

That morning Pike's legs were weak as he dressed.

"Tell me something," Sandy said, leaning her head on her hand as she watched Pike dress.

"What?"

"What would you do if I pronounced you unfit to ride?"

He stood up and said, "You didn't complain a bit last night."

"Will you come this way again?" she asked.

"Occasionally."

"Do you have other women waiting for you to come back to other settlements all over the Rockies?"

He took a moment to think and then said,

"Well, not all over the Rockies."

"Well," she said, "maybe none of them can claim what I can."

"What's that?"

"That I nursed you back to health, good as ever."

He leaned over and kissed her mouth, gently, but lingeringly.

"Mmmm," she said, "make that better than ever."

He smiled and said, "That's my girl."

THE DESTROYER
By Warren Murphy and Richard Sapir